Bonded

With

Love

With Love Series

Book 1

Tiffany Heiser

ISBN-13: 978-0-615-56805-8

PUBLISHER'S NOTE:

This is a work of fiction. Names, characters, places, and incidents either are the product of the author's imagination or are used fictitiously, and any resemblance to actual persons, living or dead, business establishments, events, or locales is entirely coincidental.

The scanning, uploading, and distribution of this book via the internet or via any other means without the permission of the publisher is illegal and punishable by law. Please purchase only authorized electronic editions, and do not participate in or encourage electronic piracy of copyrighted materials. Your support of the author's rights is appreciated.

Dedication

I want to dedicate this book to my parents, the two people who have always shown their love for me, and pushed me since the very beginning to follow my dreams. And so I have. I love you both To the Moon and Back.

To my husband for putting up with the many long days where I basically ignored you and spent my day at the computer. Thank you for helping me and believing in me. Without you my life would be incomplete. I love you forever and always.

ACKNOWLEDGMENTS

I wanted to first say thank you to the many people that helped me get through writing this novel. My best friends- Val, Tabi, and Manda - you girls have been the best. And Em-without your extra pair of eyes this would have been an epic fail. You all pushed me and helped me make this the best it could be.
To my parents, as always this step wouldn't have been taken without your guidance and love.
To my husband- you are my rock, without you I would have tumbled and fallen.
To my family and friends without you I wouldn't be me. I wouldn't be filled with love. Without you believing in me I couldn't believe in myself.
To all of you I say- thank you from the bottom of my heart.

Chapter 1

My heart reminded me to breathe when it slammed against my chest, threatening to break free. The sidewalk, only a few steps away, offered me a way out of the Texas heat but even that was too far for my shaky legs and nauseous stomach. I forced myself to pathetically lean against a tree for balance. The violent throbbing in my head caused beads of sweat to trickle down my forehead, forming a damp trail to my neck. I could barely stand- let alone walk. What the hell was wrong with me?

I snapped back to reality when Cecile grabbed my shoulders. I stared into her honey-brown eyes full with concern. "Rena what's wrong? Are you okay?"

What *was* wrong with me?

Cecile Christine Richards, my best friend since kindergarten. It all started when we joined forces to conquer the playground against all boys. She became like a sister to me and still is the closest thing I have to family.

My voice was unsure. "I don't know, maybe the heat?" I swallowed audibly. "I'm sorry I worried you." Giving a half grin and shrugging, I brushed away strands of my dark brown hair from my face then pushed off of the tree and led the way from the grounds to school.

We made our way to first period which helped calm me after the strange morning. Cecile and I shared most of our senior classes. English was one of them.

She and I lived together off of the money my parent's life insurance left me, on top of a large savings account started for my college career. My mom made sure a long time ago I would be set for a while if anything were to happen to them. The savings hadn't been touched yet, hoping one day I would be able to figure out exactly what I wanted to be when I grew up. Plus I wanted to leave this town and start a new life for myself.

Cecile's parents didn't keep track of her. She never had the best home life, with an alcoholic father, and a mother too caught up in herself- they didn't seem to care whether she came or went. When my world turned upside down she left them and stayed with me.

I whispered to her, "lucky you, getting to spend extra time with me."

"Uh, no, I'm thinking more lucky you than me." Cecile laughed loudly at her own lame comeback.

"Yeah, yeah. Did you finish the weekend reading?"

She shook her head. "I got halfway through, but was bored to tears, so I went shopping for some new shoes instead."

The final bell rang, signaling the start of class. Mrs. Dawson pulled down the projector screen and the beginning credits of *Beastly,* a new age take on *Beauty and the Beast,* rolled across the TV. My mind wandered into the main characters'. With true love's kiss, a curse being broken and a happy ending, I found myself not caring if I ended up being the beast or the unsuspecting girl. I wanted my happily ever after, like I'd read about all my life.

She is here.

The whisper made the hairs on my arms stand at attention. I surveyed the room closely, assuming I was hearing things. I shrugged it off and gave all of my focus to the movie.

Oh god she is here. It has been so long.

My thoughts paused for the whisper that startled me once again. I took my time to look around at each student. Few eyes were glued to the movie, others stayed closed as their owners napped. Not knowing where the whisper came from, I thought of all possibilities the words could mean, but that stopped when *it* hit me again.

My breath caught in my throat, icy chills filled every limb of my body, and beads of sweat formed on my brow. Breath wheezed its way out, barely crawling past my lips. Gurgling noises bubbled from my throat. What was this? Am I choking? Having a panic attack? Am I dying? Breathe, I told myself. I only needed to breathe.

Mrs. Dawson paused the movie and everyone turned in their seats. Even the nappers woke to gawk at me while I inhaled loudly. Unable to escape awkward stares from my peers, I gasped for air and filled my lungs up once again.

No one said a word, they all peered at me until Mrs. Dawson started to walk toward me. "Rena, are you alright dear?"

Cecile turned to me, her eyes watched my every move.

Coughing, I answered, "no ma'am. I think I'm coming down with something. Can I go to the nurse's office?"

She nodded her teacher nod. "Of course. I'll write you out a pass."

Hearing small murmurs from the other kids, I mashed my books into my backpack. Then took the pass for the nurse's office and fled from the room, hoping Cecile would come find me.

Lying in the dark cave-like nurse's office helped.

I dozed off, and an image snuggled behind my eyelids. The vision showed spiked raven hair bristling through my thoughts. Glowing blue eyes stared through the curtain of darkness. The image didn't scare me, I knew in my head that it was a dream, and definitely better than my embarrassing episode in Mrs. Dawson's class.

I continued to enjoy my sneak peak. Like looking through a video camera, the scene panned out and I could see more of him. His full lips turned up into a grin and swirls of emotions swam through my body at his gorgeous features. I had the urge to reach up and stroke his beautiful face, so I did. Slowly lifting my hand to brush my finger across his soft looking skin, a knocking at the door startled me. I opened my eyes and sat up, cheeks flustered.

Cecile came in with a tray of food in her hands. "I brought you lunch in bed." Her voice enthusiastically squeaked.

"Aw thanks. You didn't have to." I scooted up in bed.

"Uh, yeah I did. You're sick. Plus it gave me a reason to get away from asshole Jackson." She sat down on a chair by my bed.

Jackson was Cecile's ex and a complete douche. He had more than one opportunity to prove that he could be a good guy, but he failed miserably every time.

"What a dumb-ass. Sorry I wasn't there to keep watch for ya."

Cecile chuckled. "No problemo. I was able to dodge him and get away."

Typically I stayed quiet and really only spent time with Cecile. I've always been like that, but it became worse after the accident.

A little over a year ago, I had been in the car with my parents, when a car swerved over to our lane. This guy was going around eighty and hit us straight on-I was the only to survive.

I had a hard time bonding anymore, out of fear of losing anyone else. But when it came to screwy Jackson and the pain still showing in Cecile's eyes, I always opened my mouth and let him know where to stick his stupid apologies.

She looked so sad now, so I changed the topic. "What the hell is wrong with me, C? Am I losing my mind or something? I've never had headaches this bad. It's like a hangover from hell, except the fact that I didn't drink anything."

"You freaked me out. I thought you might pass out or choke to death or something. Are you feeling okay now?"

"Yeah, my head feels a little better, but all the nurse could give me was one lousy Tylenol- dumb-ass. Like I'm really going to OD on Tylenol. Well, thank god you're here. Now we can go."

"Oh, that sucks. You should've come and gotten the keys from me. I have to stay for cheer-leading practice tonight." She fished the keys from her purse. "Here you go, if you still feel sick later just text me and I'll get someone to take me home."

"Works for me. Thanks C."

"No problem Ren. I'm going to head out. Get some rest okay?" She patted my shoulder and gave one last glance before she closed the door behind her.

Grabbing my sunglasses and making sure the keys were in my purse, I ventured outside and made my way to her purple VW Bug. I was glad we'd snagged our parking spot closer to school this morning. I had a feeling it worked out that way so Cecile could park next to her new crush. I didn't complain since I didn't have to walk a mile through the parking lot this time.

Climbing into the bug, I felt like whatever had hit me before was gone, so I decided to head to the book store. There was always a reason to go book shopping, it made everything better.

I pulled into the parking lot of *Books City,* Granbury's local book store, and headed inside to do some damage to my bank account. I felt like being generous to myself after the weird morning.

The bell above the door jingled as I walked into the building, and the smells of new and old books wafted their way through my nostrils. This was heaven. I perused the aisles finding the new supernatural and fantasy ones. I thought about the large pile at home waiting to be read. It was about to get larger.

I made my way toward the counter to pay, when the pounding headache found its way back. Immediately following, nausea clenched my stomach causing a few gags to gurgle out of my throat. I couldn't catch my breath and my heart jabbed against my rib cage.

Trying to walk, and find somewhere to sit, I fell taking the books with me to the floor.

When my eyes opened, darkness surrounded me. One tiny light peaked from behind the black drapes. Fear tightened its grip on my stomach.

I stood on legs of jello and made my way toward the light, hoping it would wake me from this odd dream. Stumbling across the dark path, a figure draped in night stood before me. A yelp escaped from my lips. I tried to get away, but his sparkling blue eyes locked me in place. With midnight hair spiked to a perfect point, he watched me with pursed lips. His toned body towered over me.

His eyes danced along each portion of my body and I felt naked standing unguarded in front of him. In those eyes there wasn't desire but a longing, and I understood. I couldn't move, and didn't want to. For the briefest of seconds we stared at each other.

Then he took a step forward. With that one step, his body was drenched in light head to toe. I could see every detail. With that one minor step forward his whole appearance had changed drastically. He went from being a dark seductive stranger, to a hideous foul beast. His blue eyes transformed to a deep shade of red like blood coated them. His lips once so full and lush, were now pulled back into a sneer as large protruding fangs slid from his gums.

I screamed and looked around for an escape, but where do you run to in the dream world?

His hand clenched against my shoulder. He spun me around and brought my back against his tight chest. Hard stiff hands pulled my head to a tilt. I felt hot steamy breath against the crevice of my neck. Was he going to bite me? Sobbing, I tried to break free from his grasp. Hoping that death in a dream was only that, but this dream seemed so real, so alive; I didn't know what to expect.

Thrashing about I felt more hands on my shoulders, and I tried to fight back. When my eyes opened, the room was bathed in beautiful luminescence. I found myself back in the book store.

"What the..." What was that? I felt relieved to be back in the real world. That dream was frightening. So real. I could feel his hands still on my body. His hot breath stuck to my neck even in the living world.

The hands that held onto me now were the saleswoman's. Cecile, surprisingly, sat with me on the floor.

She held my head in her lap and hovered above my face. "Ren, are you okay?"

I blinked repeatedly.

The saleswoman leaned over where I laid. "I checked your phone miss, sorry, I just looked for the last person you talked to. Oh and I also called 9-1-1. I didn't know what was going on, but I'm definitely not certified for anything but CPR."

"No, no, it's fine. Thank you, but I'm fine. I just need to get home and rest. How did you get here C?" I asked huskily.

"Mason from English class brought me." Her large eyes were even wider now with fear.

"I'm fine Cecile, really. It's only been a few minutes."

"Ugh, no, you've been out for at least fifteen minutes. I made sure Mason sped over here."

A bonus about living in a small town, it only took about five minutes to get anywhere. Plus the high school sat next door to the bookstore.

I started hearing distant sirens of the ambulance, on its way to check up on me. I hoped if I stood up and acted normal, they would go away. Raising myself off of Cecile's lap, my head rushed with blood but I forced myself to stand.

"Hey the ambulance is almost here, I don't think you should get up." The saleswoman put her hand on my shoulder.

I caught sight of her name tag. "Darla, I'm fine. I just need to go home and relax. C, will you please take me home? Seriously I'm better." I did a little jig in the middle of the aisle, only to prove I could without toppling over, but the dizziness lingered. The room began to spin and I quickly regretted moving at all.

"Okay fine Ren, I will take you home, but I will be on your butt in two seconds if I sense even one thing wrong with you. Got it?"

I rolled my eyes. "Yeah got it." Turning, I said, "thanks for your help Darla, and so sorry for the scare. I'll let them do their check-up before we go home."

She nodded.

I begrudgingly waited to get checked on by the paramedics, and once they gave me a clean bill of health we headed home.

I had hoped for a little more from my senior year, but this pushed limits.

* * * * * * * * *

"Rena come one. We're late." Cecile called.

The last one out as always, I grabbed a strawberry pop-tart and bolted to Cecile's bug.

She peeled out of the driveway and flew at a speed that caused the purple bug to growl in protest.

Trying to mentally wake up, I made an unintelligible comment. "I slept in, sorry."

"S'kay, no big. I had told Mason and Jen we would meet them by the fountain."

"Oh, who's Jen? And why are we meeting them?"

"We need to decide on our presentation for Mrs. Dawson's class, and they offered to be paired up with us. Most likely thanks to your super brainpower."

Rolling my eyes, I mumbled, "oh okay. Sorry again. I had a rough night."

"Is it the headaches? Or are you still having those nightmares?"

"Its nightmares. The headaches haven't come back since yesterday morning."

"Wanna talk about it?" she asked.

"It's all the same stuff. Just the same awful scenes, C." Tears stung the corners of my eyes, replaying the images from last night's nightmare.

We stopped at a red light and she turned to look at me.

I tried blinking away the tears pooling around the edges of my eyes. "I had hoped they would go away, but my counselor said they wouldn't for a while. She said the guilt I feel definitely isn't helping."

"Ren, you have absolutely nothing to feel guilty about. I've told you that, everyone has. It wasn't your fault at all."

"But I was the only one, Cecile. I must have done something different to still be alive and for them to be dead. If I would've known what kept me alive, I could have warned my family."

She shook her head. "It was that son-of-a-bitch, the one that fell asleep at the wheel, who did this to you and your parents. It wasn't your fault."

"I guess. Maybe that's why I'm still having nightmares. I can't get my mind to wrap around it, only around what I could have done to prevent it." The pooling tears spilled over. I couldn't stop them. No one could say anything to make me feel any different.

Cecile wiped at her eyes too. The memories were fresh in my mind.

Dark clouds puckered with rain above us. Splashes of raindrops covered the windshield, with the weather on the verge of becoming Spring. Driving home from an aunt's house, my parents sat in the front seats singing a duet of some lame rock song. I watched an alien crash through New York in the movie playing on the DVD player. Out of nowhere blinding beams of light shot through the car, followed by the sound of squealing tires exploding all around us. Mom screamed.

I passed out and then woke lying in a hospital bed, alone. One leg simply bandaged, the other in a cast and throbbing with pain. It felt like hours until a doctor finally stopped by to do a basic check-up. She also broke the devastating news; my family was dead.

"We're here." Cecile's words brought me back.

The sun shone brightly in the sky. We marched through the grassy fields covering the front of school. The heat showed its strength early this morning, flexing its muscles by throwing large amounts of dry hot wind in our faces.

We made our way toward the fountain to meet Mason and Jen, and Cecile explained why we had parked in a different spot this week. "Okay, so I've met someone new."

"I figured that was the reason we parked so close now. Not that I'm complaining. Who is he?"

"His name is Drake, he's absolutely stunning. Bronze hair that he fixes into that messy-just-got-outta-bed look, you know what I'm talking about?"

"Uh-huh, like every other guy in this school. Is he a senior?"

"I think so."

"Where'd he come from?"

"Dunno. But he's got amazing gray eyes, and he's tall. Plus he has a hot body." I could practically hear the slobber dripping from her lips. "And he drives that completely hot looking blue mustang."

"Have y'all talked?"

"Nope, but I'm working on it. I have all these awesome plans on how to catch his attention."

"Oh this should be good. So what are your 'awesome' plans?" Without intending to, sarcasm jumped from my mouth.

She ignored it. "Okay, so what if I try the bend and snap?"

"That's from *Legally Blonde*."

"So? It worked for that one lady."

"As long as you can control your snap." I stifled a giggle,as she continued.

"What if I knock my pen off the corner of the desk in class as he walks by, and then when he hands it to me we stare lovingly into each others eyes?"

"Seriously? *That's Clueless.* You better hope he doesn't turn out gay for your sake. Don't you have any of your own material?"

"That's it. That's all I got." She had stopped walking, and now stared at me with her arms crossed, a pout forming on her lips. "What do you suggest then, miss smart-ass?"

"I would go with 'Hi', or even 'Hello'. I know it seems strange and less cheesy but lots of guys fall for it." I laughed hard.

"Oh whatever. Hey there's Mason and Jen." She waved and jogged toward our friends.

Trying to keep up with her, I made it halfway when I felt *it* all over again. The headache was back at full force.

"Not again..." I squeaked, before chills broke through my entire system.

I immediately felt an arm wrapped around me from behind as I drifted to the ground. My body was brought down slowly and my head laid comfortably on someone's legs. The smell of pine trees filled my nostrils. I was mildly aware of talking going on around me.

My vision blurred and I tried to clear it up by blinking, but it didn't work. A fog covered my sight but a voice rang clear as a bell in my head.

Soft, yet masculine. It whispered so close to my ear. "Oh my love, I have waited so long for you." The voice sounded familiar.

"Wh...who are you?" Fear crept through me, but I was too weak to do anything except lay there.

"Do not fear dear one. I will take care of you." The strange whisper shimmered through my mind.

A cup touched my lips. My dry throat screamed for whatever liquid filled it. Weakness filled me and I lay too disoriented to object. A fruity scent drifted toward me, causing my mouth to water and I drank the sweet flavored juice that spilled into my mouth.

"You will feel better once you drink." The voice whispered once again.

The arm around me tightened. The juice stopped flowing and the cup pulled from my lips.

In seconds, the fog had lifted and my vision cleared. A face bent over me and I found myself staring into a pair of sparkling blue eyes.

Chapter 2

My heart thrummed in my eardrums staring at his face and into his amazing blue eyes. My eyes trailed over every facial feature, every perfect angle of his jaw, and lush full lips that sat in a grin. His face was familiar, but it's impossible that he had been in my dreams.

I tried using my own get-a-guy-tactics that I tried to teach Cecile earlier. "Um...Hi." Very smooth.

A soft melodious voice traveled to my ears. "Hello, Rena."

Still sprawled out in his arms, I hopped up. My eyes stayed on his. It felt like a trance kept our eyes locked. "How'd you know my name?"

A smile formed on his lips, and I had to keep myself from melting into a giant puddle of hormones in front of him. "People talk," he shrugged. "I am Cryder by the way."

"Oh. Nice to meet you." Standing up quickly, dizziness took over and I started to fall again, but stopped when his arms wrapped around me. Butterflies waged wars against each other in my stomach, and I could feel heat simmering on my face as my eyes remained on those dazzling blues. He looked like *him*, but there's no way, right?

He helped me up, but held onto my shoulders making sure I wouldn't fall again. His hard stiff hands crept down my arms. "Well, it is definitely a pleasure to meet you Rena. I'm sure I'll see you again," Cryder said and he dipped his head toward me.

It is him!

My mouth rushed my brain as I realized who he was. "Me-see-too-you-soon-again-soon." That was my cue to walk away, and so I did. I spun around to head in the complete opposite direction of Cryder, groups of girls watched us.

Their stares held a lot of confusion. But when Cryder locked into their sight, their looks transformed to desire, and suddenly girly giggles swirled in the air. I felt like jumping into his arms and waving mine, shouting, "he's mine! I found him first!" But chastised myself for falling to the drama girls' level. Glancing back, I hoped to get one more glimpse of his enchanting face, but he had vanished. His exit left a stinging in my chest. I felt pathetic, letting it affect me so much. I began to make my trek to class, but then Cecile jumped in front of my path.

Startling me. "So, what happened?"

"Nothing, we just said 'Hi', I mumbled, then walked away as fast as possible." Uncertain if my mind could handle talking about my dream man coming to life.

Cecile followed me. "What happened to all that great advice you gave me?"

"Well, I said 'Hi' didn't I?"

She rolled her eyes. "Anyway, I was asking about why you were on the ground to begin with."

"Chills and a headache. Do you think it could just be the heat causing all of this? Or do you think there really is something wrong with me, C?" A worried tone filled my voice.

"It's not something wrong with you, just a reaction from everything you've been through. We'll figure it all out. Promise."

She patted my shoulder in a comforting gesture. "So, did you know him?"

"Who?" I asked, as a smirk formed on my lips. How could I not know him, or his name?

"Cryder, Drake's cousin. The guy who had his hands all over you?"

"No. I didn't really know him. That's Drake's cousin?" She nodded. "How do you know him?"

"Oh, Jen gave me the scoop over by the fountain. I was asking about Drake, of course, but then we saw you and Cryder getting all sorts of cozy. So I asked about him too."

"I think I've seen him before, but I'm not sure where." I decided against confessing about my dreams, and Cryder being in them, until I felt absolutely certain. It was going to sound crazy no matter what, but I wanted to be one hundred percent positive.

"Well he looked pretty comfortable around you." She winked.

"Oh, please. He just was there when my body decided to go crazy again."

"Does it seem like it's getting worse?"

"Yeah, it does, and it kinda scares me. I think I'm going to set up an appointment for the doc, just to get checked out."

"Okay. I think you need to go, it seems like it's getting worse to me." Her usual look of concern was back, as she stared at me for a few seconds.

The class bell rang, cuing the end of our conversation. We walked down the hallway.

I kept glancing behind me, hoping to see Cryder again before we went into class, but he wasn't anywhere around.

Biology class started, and I pictured those dreamy blue eyes for a split second and they sent tingles to my stomach. Thinking about the beautiful smile he had on his gorgeous face, sent a shiver swimming up my spine. I was brought back to the real world when I noticed everyone's eyes on me. Mr. Pyler, my teacher, stood next to my desk. He apparently had been saying my name this whole time.

Short gray-haired Mr. Pyler, gestured his head toward his hand, which held a folded up piece of notebook paper. "It appears Ms. Vesten, you have dropped this note."

I stared at him blankly, and Mr. Pyler tapped his foot on the tiled floor. A sure tone filled my voice. "That's not mine, sir. People don't pass notes anymore, we text. Writing notes is for the old timers." Bad timing for a sarcastic comment.

"And bad form to pick up a chick." Some guy from across the room mumbled under his breath.

Mr. Pyler turned toward the direction of the guy, then back to me and flipped the note over. There written in beautiful penmanship, was my name. "Take it now, or I will read it in front of everyone. And you better watch your tone with me, or I will be glad to offer detention for that mouth of yours."

I snatched the note from his hand, feeling the heat from embarrassment grow warmer in my cheeks. "Um, thank you sir."

He pursed his lips. "If you don't mind, I would like to continue with class, and please do not litter my walkway again."

I nodded, as he stomped back to the front of class. After everything else that had gone wrong, this week needed to be over soon.

Staring at my name written in pretty calligraphy on the outside of the note, I picked it up, and brought it to my lap. Opening it, I first searched at the bottom of the page for a name, anything to give a clue to who had sent it, but there was none. I sat confused why someone would write a note, instead of text, it seemed almost archaic.

Again, no one jumped up and down waving their hands to confess about writing the note, or embarrassing me in the middle of class. I did notice a new student though, and wondered if he was the "hot" guy Cecile talked about. Cryder's cousin, Drake. I stared at the letter, the sentence actually, reading it over multiple times in my head.

Your blood is mine.

There was one sentence on the whole paper. My hands shook and my breath came in shallow gasps. The room around me started to go blurry and my knees began to tremble. I jumped out of my desk and hurtled myself through the classroom door, not caring who stared.

Once I made my way to the bathroom I locked the door behind me. Shaking, I splashed water on my face to calm down. I read the note once more, turning it around and checking again that my name was still on the outside. I couldn't deny it. This one sentence was intended for my eyes only. The words scrambled around and around in my head, making me sick to my stomach. A dozen different emotions brought on by only a few words.

* * * * * * * * *

Heading outside for lunch, I found Cecile sitting in our normal spot; a bench by the fountain. We'd claimed that spot since we were freshman.

As complete opposites, we still managed to stay attached at the hip. Where she normally wore pastel pinks and pale purples with heels to accentuate her gazelle-like legs, my outfits consisted of tees and extra comfortable jeans. The loose clothing hid the curves that matured rapidly on my vertically challenged frame, without asking for my permission first. In my vain attempt to receive eye contact with the guys, I kept the *girls* fully-covered.

We normally sat together, just the two of us. Instead of sitting and waiting for me today, she sat with the new student, Drake.

She noticed me standing there, and glided over in one smooth motion. "What happened, sweetheart? You just shot out of class after Mr. Pyler gave you that note." Cecile placed her arms around my shoulders and directed me to sit on the bench with the new kid.

"Started feeling sick is all. Apparently Mr. Pyler decided to tattle on me, because there was banging on the bathroom door in less than five minutes, and I had to go in and sit with Mrs. Stanley."

"The principal? No way. What did she have to say?"

"That my behavior was uncalled for, and I better never do it again."

With a roll of her eyes. "That's it? Any other student, and they would've gotten a month of detention. But not you, Miss Brainiac. Are you feeling sick still?"

"Not right now. It comes and goes."

"Well I'm keeping my eyes on you, and I'm about two seconds away from dragging your ass to the hospital. You're really worrying me."

"Let's just get through this day. "Kay?" In a stern voice.

"Fine. I guess, Rena. But if it doesn't go away by this afternoon, I'm yanking you by the hair to the hospital. Got it?" I nodded. "So what did the note say that had you all riled up?"

I gulped loudly and hoped like hell she didn't hear it. "This had nothing to do with the note. I was...in the bathroom. Seriously." I hesitated, not wanting to spill my dramatic guts in front of the new guy.

But his golden-gray eyes stayed on Cecile, following her every move. At my comment, Drake turned to me with a knowing smile. "In Biology? That was extremely awkward between you and Mr. Pyler. I was glad to be sitting in the back and no where near his glare." His whole body was turned toward me now.

"Did you...never-mind...Yeah it was."

"I didn't see where it came from, but I bet it was an important note, to interrupt class like that." His voice held a knowing tone, as if trying to coax me to say more.

"Oh, it just had a sentence. And it didn't make any sense." I gave a slight shrug, trying to act nonchalant, even though inside I was shaking.

"I see." Again his tenor voice held a tone like he knew my secret. His eyes stayed on mine for a brief second, before transferring to Cecile.

Cecile, obviously feeling left out, went to wrap her arms around him as if staking claim. That was odd behavior for her. "Where are my manners?" Her voice was extra squeaky. "Drake this is my best friend in the whole wide world, Rena Marie Vesten. Rena, this is Drake Leone, our new student from...where are you from again?"

As if I hadn't known his name or heard all about him already, I said. "nice to meet you Drake." We shook hands.

He was a thin guy, with a long torso and lanky legs. He had bronzed shaggy hair, the color of a penny, and thin lips that quirked up in a half grin every now and then. His eyes glowed with yellow sunbursts speckled in the pupils.

"Nice to meet you as well Rena." A smile replaced his grin, and it looked better on his face than the smirk I caught earlier. "Ah yes, and I am from Bloomsburg, Pennsylvania." He sounded old-fashioned, especially for an eighteen year old boy.

"Wow, you moved all the way from up north to as far down south as you could go, huh? So, why'd you move?" Cecile asked.

"Well," he started. "My cousin and I decided that the town we lived in was becoming over-populated with controlling family members. They have different wishes for our futures, and so we came here."

"So you live alone? So do we," Cecile enthusiastically announced.

"Is that so?" Drake asked.

The bell rang to indicate lunch had ended.

I gathered up my backpack from the ground and grabbed onto Cecile's arm. "Let's go, we've got class to get to."

"We can stay a little longer." Her starry eyes focused on Drake.

"It's Mrs. Lane, and I've heard tardiness equals extra work in her class. Plus, I've already gotten in trouble once today, I don't want to add to it. Let's go, please?" She finally stood up. "Nice meeting you Drake, hope we get to talk more." I threw over my shoulder as we walked toward the building.

In the distance, a whisper floated on the wind from his direction. "Oh you will."

Something wasn't right with the cousins from P.A. Their speech and the way they carried themselves, didn't fit the teenager's norm. And behind the golden flecks in their eyes, sat a long sad history. A past that went far beyond their claimed eighteen years of existence.

Chapter 3

Cecile raved about Drake all morning. Going to class let me get away from the holiness that was Drake, since according to Cecile he was sent to her from god. Once class ended though, I knew it would all start again. I leaned against the locker door in defeat waiting until Cecile's bouncing blonde curls headed in my direction.

Her laughter filled the hallway, as she walked toward me from class. I waved enthusiastically to get her attention, but my hand immediately dropped when I saw Drake walking beside her. He had been the cause of her over-zealous laughter.

She came to stand next to me. "Oh hey Rena, what's going on? Drake was just telling me the funniest story ever."

Forcing a smile on my face, I falsely responded. "Great. I'd love to hear it some time."

"Well, maybe he can tell you all about it in the car- we're dropping him off at home." A questionable look filled my eyes, which she dismissed as she grabbed Drake's hand and headed to the parking lot.

I ran to catch up with them, then whispered in Cecile's ear, "why does he need a ride? Doesn't he drive that blue car?" Tilting my head in Drake's direction.

Drake leaned forward and stared at me in the eyes. Had he heard me? "Yes, the mustang is mine. However, I let Cryder borrow it because he said he had errands to run and whatnot. So, Cecile was generous enough to offer me a ride."

We continued to walk, and Cecile laughed at every word that came out of his mouth. Maybe I was over-reacting, but something about him, and his whole demeanor didn't sit right with me.

I followed behind them and backed away before the two made me sick.

Making it to the car, I reached down to open the passenger side door, and was stopped by a hand on my shoulder. Twirling around, Drake and I were face-to-face. It took every ounce of control to keep from throwing his hand off my shoulder. I stared into his eyes not backing down. His hot breath singed my cheek.

He opened his mouth and spoke. "I know the answers to your questions." Still staring into his eyes, I held my trembling hands behind my back. "However, the answers will not be given if you don't prove to Cecile that we can play nicely." He forced a smile, but behind his facade was a threat.

A lump of fear formed in my throat, but I swallowed it down. "We'll see. Friendship is earned Drake. And there is *a lot* to be earned right now." I turn toward Cecile fuming. A cloudy red haze formed over my eyes. I blinked a few times and took a deep breath. The haze floated away. "I'm going to walk home, C."

A confused look formed on Cecile's face. "Why?"

I slowly shook my head. "I need fresh air. And," twisting my head back to face Drake as I said, "I'm just not ready to play nice." I stomped away.

Cecile called my name and it floated on the wind following my trail, but I kept walking. Wanting to get away from Drake and his arrogance, I let my legs carry me out of the parking lot and down the hill toward Main Street. I knew it would take a while to make it home, but it would be better than dealing with the very awkward car ride with Mr. all-knowing and my robotic best friend.

Cecile followed him everywhere now, stayed by his side, and left me to wander alone. The walk home became a pity party, with only one guest-me.

Drake's words swam through my mind, along with his smirk. With his constant talk about my note, he must have known who wrote it or maybe even what he words meant. What other answers could he have? Did he know about my dreams, and the ones I had of Cryder? There's no possible way he could, I hadn't told anyone.

Shaking the thoughts from my head, I made my way to Main Street wondering why I had worn pants today. Texas was great, but the summers were ridiculous. Even at the end of August heading into the Fall the temp stayed in the nineties. Trees and flowers died, yards stayed brown, and sweat trickled the second you stepped outside. I stepped of the curb to cross over from Main to Doyle, when a honk shattered my eardrums.

Startled, I bounced back, in time to get out of the way from a...blue mustang. Mixed emotions stirred in my stomach. There were plenty of blue mustangs in town, it couldn't be Cryder. I squinted, trying to see inside the car, but I couldn't see anything through the overly tinted windows. I attempted to step down again, when the passenger side window rolled down. The driver of this blue mustang, leaned over and stared at me. Watching me with eyes matching the car he drove. Cryder sat behind the wheel.

"You need a ride?" His sweet voice caressed my ears.

"Um...well...I was just going home." Good conversationalist, that's what I was.

"You look hot. I mean you're sweaty. I mean...it's hot outside, isn't it?"

I chuckled. He looked as nervous as I felt. Biting my lip, I contemplated whether I should jump in the car with him. But he looked so sweet sitting there, plus questions needed to be asked, and now would be the best time.

"Sounds good to me," I smiled.

"Good." He smiled back, and the gold in his eyes became more visible.

Cryder effortlessly climbed out of the sports car, and came to where I stood to open my door. Then graciously removed my backpack from my shoulder and I slid into the seat.

We drove for a couple of minutes and I gave him instructions to my house. Besides that the car ride stayed quiet.

I finally tried to start an actual conversation. "So, where did you and your cousin live before?"

"A town in the mountains of Pennsylvania. Have you always lived in Granbury?"

"Yes. Born and raised. Boring huh?"

"Not at all. This town is great. Especially compared to where I came from."

"Was it that bad?"

"Not really the town, more our large family that surrounded us. They expected a lot from me, as well as from Drake, and we didn't want that anymore."

"So, you just left your family behind?" Sadness filled his eyes, and his grip tightened on the steering wheel. I decided to change the topic. "Where at in Granbury do y'all live?"

"We are on the outskirts, living in that house on the hill." I gasped, and he turned to glance at me. "Are you alright?"

"Um...yes. You live in the Conti house? I'm surprised anyone lives there. It's so eerie. I've even heard it's haunted." My hands wrapped around my seat belt, thinking about all of the scary stories I've heard.

Not too long ago a kid Cecile and I knew from school, Daniel, went into the house and when he came out he had completely changed. Before he stepped foot in there he had been sane and a genius, but now he was barely passing. Rumor around school was that the ghost got to him and erased his memory. That place terrified me.

"Well, I do know a few people have died there, but when you are basically given a house, it is terribly rude to say no."

My eyes went as wide as saucers. "Gave you the house?"

"Yes, that house belongs to my family, and has for many generations. When Drake and I talked about moving, my Grandfather suggested that we move here, and make the house into our new home. He knew it would be wise for us to leave when we did, and start new lives. So, nice to meet you I'm Cryder Conti." His grip loosened on the wheel, and he put his hand out for me to shake.

I shook it. "Turn left at the next road, on Morgan. My house is the third on the right. It was basically given to me also."

"Oh, really? How so?"

"My parents...are...they." I couldn't say it. "Well, my dad left for work, and so my mom went to be with him. It is only for a short period of time, and I couldn't go because of school, so I stayed and live there with Cecile."

"Where are Cecile's parents?"

"At their house. She left them." I left it at that, as we pulled onto my driveway. "Thanks for the ride, Cryder." That name slid off my tongue so easily, and it tasted so sweet.

"Here let me help you." He got out and came to my side, to open my door, again. He then leaned forward and gave me his hand, and helped me out of the car. "I'll carry that for you." Grabbing my backpack, he slung it over his shoulder, and we made our way to the house.

I stood on my tip-toes to peak through the garage making sure Cecile was inside. I had left my keys at home, since I thought we would be riding together.

Cryder had already made his way onto the porch, and he set my backpack down on the porch swing. This would be another awkward moment, I could tell already.

"So, thanks again. Maybe we can do it again sometime, but without the whole almost running over me thing?"

He laughed nervously. "Absolutely. I would enjoy that. I heard that you had some crazy stalker sent you a note in one of your classes today. Are you okay?"

"You heard about that?" I asked. "Small town can be annoying sometimes," I mumbled.

"Well if you are having problems with some guy, I'd be glad to help you out of it."

"That's sweet, but I'm not sure what the note really meant. It was kind of creepy, but it could have been a prank. Who knows?"

"Well if it gets worse let me know."

"Thank you." I placed my hand on his arm.

Our eyes met, and just like in the sappy movies, everything happened in slow motion. He started to lean toward me. Goosebumps rose on my skin. He closed his eyes, and his lips puckered. The desire to be with him, near him, and to never leave pulled at me. But on the other hand, a voice yelled loudly in my head that something wasn't right. I could feel my eyes closing, ready to embrace the soft feel of his lips on mine. The safe voice could stuff it for all I cared. I wanted him.

I copied his movements, closing my eyes, puckering my lips, and feeling my heart race out of control. The kiss, about to happen with our lips only inches apart, when a high-pitched very annoying voice sliced our moment in half.

Cecile stood at the door with both her hands on her hips. "Where have you been? I need to talk to you now." And as if she hadn't spotted Cryder before, her eyes went wide and her demeanor changed. "Oh, hi Cryder. Sorry, I didn't see you there." How could she not?

"Yeah, he's here, and I'm here. We are here, standing on the porch together, and *alone*." That last word emphasized, trying to get her to walk away, but it didn't work.

She glanced over at me, then back at Cryder. "I dropped Drake off earlier, he said he would be expecting you soon. I need to talk with my bestie. So, we will see you tomorrow, Cryder."

He nodded. "Very well. I will see you both tomorrow."

I followed after him a few steps. "You don't have to leave." Yes, he does, because the grip he had on me earlier was growing.

"Yes, I should go. Have a good night."

"You too." I turned away from him, but glared into the unnerved eyes of Cecile.

The second I stepped through the doorway, Cecile started griping. "I hope you'll be more like the friend I know tomorrow, because today I didn't like how you were acting. It was embarrassing and rude."

"He came at me and..."

She walked through the foyer to the den, and sat on our brown leather love seat. "He only wants to be friends."

I followed her into the room but stayed standing. "He scared me, then demanded that I be his friend. That's not how it works. And now I don't like your 'tude. You're becoming obsessed, and you just met him."

"I've heard enough."

"No, I don't think you have. Until he acts normal and not like a creeper, then I'll be more accepting."

"Be nice to him, please. I really like him and I don't want anything to screw it up." She said with tear filled eyes.

"Are you crying? You've never been this way especially toward a guy, and especially toward me. You need to chill."

"Sorry, I don't know what's gotten into me." Large raindrop tears splashed down her face.

"What's up with the mood swings? First you're mad, now you're sad? What is it about him that's making you act that way?"

"I don't know. I just have this feeling like I need to be with him. And when he's around, no one else matters." Her shoulders shook noticeably, as she took a deep breath. "But you're right, I've never acted this way before. Its kinda weird, but I really do like him."

"It's too soon, don't you think? I mean you..." I shut up, because I felt like a hypocrite. My mind immediately turned to Cryder as I spoke. "Never mind, you are old enough to know what you want, just be careful. 'Kay?

"Alright. I'll try. Sorry."

"It's fine. We all get that way at some point." Cryder's face hid behind my eyelids, still reminding me of the secret I kept.

* * * * * * * * *

The next morning started off just like any other, until I realized Drake was now a member of our little secluded group, and with group- I meant Cecile and me.

With the sun high in the sky, and the heat tormenting everyone who tried to walk through it, we decided to eat lunch inside. Drake and Cecile sat opposite of me at our table, making googly eyes. I sat quietly.

Drake turned to me with a sly smile. "Have you met my cousin, Cryder, yet?"

"Oh yeah, Rena has most definitely met him. He came to her rescue the other day. Everyone saw them out on the grounds." Cecile answered for me.

"Yeah, I've met him. He helped me out, but that was all." With an uncaring shrug, I bit into my sandwich.

"I've been getting all the info on Cryder, and he sounds absolutely perfect for you." Cecile gushed.

I turned to Drake. "Well where is he? How come he doesn't sit with us?"

As I stood to throw my trash away, Drake pointed behind me. "Ah, speak of the devil himself. Here he comes now."

I turned to see that captivating face again, but my body began to tremble. Starting with my hands, a strong shiver controlled my body. I collapsed to the ground, feeling a scream bubbling at my throat, and I prayed it wouldn't get worse. But it did. The migraine attacked again, and my stomach clenched with pain. Everything hit at once, and the darkness clouded my vision. Then a soft yet deep, and soothing voice spoke to me. It whispered through my mind.

Now is the true beginning, I will not let go. She is mine.

This voice was one I remembered. A familiar sound, I couldn't place, but right then it didn't matter as darkness took over.

For brief moments, my eyes would open to the sunlight. Glimpses of an angular chin, pursed full lips, and eyes furrowed in concentration popped into my vision. At one point, that face transformed into the terrifying beast I had seen once in a dream. Sharp fangs protruding from gums, stabbed into *those* lips, and as I kept staring, blood red eyes turned down and focused on me. I couldn't tell between dream or reality, but I was helpless to react.

Those stunning facial features belonged to one person, and I had seen him in my dreams as well. The soothing voice, gorgeous face, the haunting whispers, blood red eyes, and pointy fangs; these all were connected by one. It hit me then, that my dreams had been invaded, by Cryder. That was impossible.

* * * * * * * * * *

"Ow." My body felt stiff.

Where was I? My eyes crept open to find darkness, and an ache throughout my body. A pillow laid comfortably underneath my head, and a thick soft blanket cocooned me.

I felt around the bed, searching for clues. My fingers bumped into a table sitting beside me. On it, I found a hard cover book and a cup that felt cool to the touch, which tempted my parched throat. Wrapping my fingers around the cup, I drained the contents.

The juice splashed against my taste-buds, tasting of freshly picked strawberries and some different sour flavor. The mixture blended perfectly and I gulped down every drop.

Attempting to sit up, I heard a noise that caused me to falter, and I collapsed back into bed. The door opened, then closed immediately with a click. My heart raced as footsteps moved closer toward me. I couldn't see a thing in the darkness. I blinked repeatedly hoping that my eyes would adjusted, but that didn't work.

Finally a whisper swished from my mouth. "Who's there?"

The other person in the room moved closer. My pulse pounded in my ears. Then I heard the voice soft like fingers tracing my skin. "It is me Rena, Cryder Conti. I came to see how you are doing."

Chills vibrated through me, although I didn't know if they were from fear or excitement. "Oh, hi. Sorry, I couldn't see you. I feel better thanks. Do you know where I'm at?"

"Hood County Hospital."

"Oh where's Cecile and Drake? I was with them."

"They are out in the waiting room. We've been here all afternoon, waiting for you to wake."

"All of you? Did they say what's going on with me?"

"Yes we couldn't leave until we all knew you were feeling better. According to the doctors you're anemic."

"What? That doesn't even sound right. I've never had problems before."

"I don't know, that's what the nurses told us." He shrugged. "I'll get a nurse to come in once I leave."

"I just want to go, I hate hospitals. They freak me out, especially ever since the...never mind."

His footsteps came closer to the bed. "Oh, the accident? Yes I am very sorry to hear about that." A sad tone filled his soft voice.

I felt my lips quiver. "How did you know about that?"

"As I said before, people talk. I am sorry, I should not have said anything."

There was a snap, then light flooded the room, from a lamp at the foot of the bed. I squinted, to adjust to the light. When my eyes finally opened, I found myself at eye level with Cryder's torso. Which was completely drool worthy.

"I uh...yeah...I dunno." Him standing there took the words right out of my mouth, and I sounded like a bumbling idiot.

I continued to stare at his frame. He was tall with broad shoulders, and his arms rippled with muscles. Immediately I felt the desire to run my fingertips up and down his arms, but I held back. He had a broad chest as well, and again I had to fight the urge to touch. Loose fitted khakis hugged tightly by a belt exhibited his small waist.

I sat there staring at his body, and when I realized it I snapped my head up to his face. He was enchanting. Everything about him caused a yearning I had never felt before, and it made me blush. His big blue eyes had beautiful long eyelashes. Each time he blinked they seemed to flap like dark wings. I could see golden flecks in them shining with the light. They glowed even brighter than a star in the night sky.

Taking another step closer, this time to the side of the bed, he stood next to me. The craving to touch him caused my fingers to ache, and I forced my self-control do its job with his eyes a few inches from mine.

Instead of being the crystal blues, they flamed a cherry red. Trying to look away, my eyes ended up on his lips, and I saw fangs again- long and deadly.

I blinked rapidly, yet the image stayed. "What...are you?"

A look of fear swam through his eyes, there for a split second then gone just as quickly.

"What do you mean?" He asked, and the terrifying image erased itself from his facial features.

"The red eyes, and fangs. I saw them. Just tell me, please. What are you? Did you write the note, or know who did it?" The pleading in my voice surprised even me. A fear had risen deeper in me, deeper than I had ever felt, and yet I longed to be held by his arms.

His eyes darted to the door, back to me. "I don't know what you are talking about. I will leave you to your rest." With those words, he fled.

Shortly after Cecile and Drake came walking into my room. Drake's mouth held a smug grin, showing he knew my secrets.

Chapter 4

A nurse stormed into the room while Cecile slowly crept in on her tip toes and sat in the chair next to my bed.

Out of breath the nurse asked, "is everything okay in here? Was that guy bothering you?"

"Uh, no, it's fine. Just a disagreement. I'm alright now." I shrugged and offered an apologetic grin. How was I suppose to explain what I just saw? Especially, how could I describe it and not be sent to the looney bin?

She eyed me suspiciously. "Alright, as long as everything is fine." The nurse walked from the room, casting one final glance at us before she closed the door behind her.

I tried to sit up, but faltered and fell back to the mattress. Startled, Cecile jumped up and stood beside the bed while I tried again. I started to fall, but two strong hands held me in place. Initially I wanted to jerk my arm away. Seeing Cryder's face change made me jumpy. Instead of screaming, like I wanted to, I twisted my head to the side and found Drake standing beside me.

I took a deep breath. "Let me...try myself." I mumbled. Drake let go and I immediately fell back to the bed.

Cecile's eyes shimmered with frustration. "Don't be stubborn, Ren. He's only trying to help." She moved to stand at Drake's side.

I had the urge to say, 'good robot', but I held it in. "I'm sorry, I just want outta this hospital. I sorta hate them, ya know?" I responded sarcastically.

Cecile's eyebrows creased. "Oh, right, sorry." Seriously? How could she not remember? She whispered to Drake, "sweetie, can you bring me my drink?"

"Did either one of you see Cryder?" I asked.

Drake walked around to the foot of my bed. "Yes. He ran out of here without one word to us. Why? He made his way to the small table near my bed, and picked up a clear plastic cup filled with a slushy red liquid- the only color I ever saw anymore.

"Well did you see his eyes? His teeth?" I asked.

Drake stopped dead in his tracks, but within seconds continued walking toward Cecile. "No. I didn't pay any attention to his teeth or his eyes. He did look very upset. Did you go and break my poor overly-sensitive cousin's heart?"

"How could I have done that? We just met. And it's been weird since the beginning." I kept my eyes focused on Drake.

He went to his bag from the corner of the room and pulled out a water bottle. The same red juice sloshed around in the bottle, and the same exact scent floated through the room as he filled the cup for Cecile. "It's been weird?" He chuckled and then continued. "You probably looked at him wrong. Who knows?"

I stared directly at Cecile. "Did you see anything different about Cryder?"

She gulped loudly, and pulled the cup from her lips. Silence dominated the room. A droplet rolled from her chin to the ground, and reverberated like surround sound in my ears. A vibrant red stain formed along the cream colored tile, and a strong strawberry smell drifted through the air. The scent enticed my senses. My mouth watered with the aroma, and my stomach rumbled with want. I balled the bed sheets up into my hands trying to hide the craving growing deep inside me.

"No, I didn't see a thing." Her gaze traveled between Drake and me.

"Well, maybe it was my imagination playing tricks on me?" I asked.

"That could be it, Ren." She said as her eyes darted everywhere around the room except at me.

I shook my head slowly, and realized what I had just said. "No. I've seen this before. On him. I know I have. In my dreams. When he was carrying me, and after I passed out. I remember these things. It was him."

"Well, what...what have you seen?" Cecile's voice shook.

I tried to concentrate on her questions, but my thoughts continued to be sucked in by the sweet succulent smell of strawberries. "What is that stuff?" I pointed to the cup in Drake's hands.

Drake stood next to Cecile now, and offered her the juice filled cup. He turned away from her in a swift motion to face me. "It is a family recipe, so to speak." He grinned. "And what's in your family recipe?" I asked.

"Well, it's strawberries, which I'm sure you have noticed by now, mixed with a secret ingredient." He winked at me.

"A secret ingredient?" Drake nodded. "Well, what is it?" I questioned.

"Oh, deary, it's a secret for a reason." He smirked.

His words left an icky feeling in the pit of my stomach. I knew Cecile didn't see it, but he definitely had a hand in Cryder's weirdness. What was the secret ingredient, and why couldn't he say anything? My mind ran wild with thoughts of what the secret ingredient could be. Could it be some kind of drug to make us fall for them? It was working on Cecile already.

"So, anyway," Drake broke through my thoughts. "What is it that you see in these visions?"

I stared directly at him. "His eyes went all red, and he had fangs. I've seen this once before. Even in my dreams. Does that make sense?"

"So, you are saying Cryder is the man of your dreams?" Drake laughed hard.

Anger clenched the blood in my veins. "It's not funny. I'm scared. Ugh, I knew I shouldn't have said anything about my dreams. Whatever. Since that's out, might as well mention I've been hearing a voice too."

Drake's head snapped into attention and focused his eyes solely on me. "Who's voice are you hearing? Are you sure you're not just going crazy?"

My hands shook from frustration. "No, I'm not going crazy. I know now. It all has something to do with you and Cryder. There is something wrong with the two of you." In a blink of an eye Drake stood beside me. With his hands on my shoulders, he pushed me down onto the bed.

"Let me go!" I struggled against his hold, thrashing about like a tree in a tornado.

His grip tightened on my shoulders, pinning me. "Answer my questions," he snarled. "And I will let you go."

Cecile stepped forward and pull him off of me. "Back off! Let her go. You're letting this go too far."

He spun his head around to look at her, and a growl escaped his lips. "Step back now. This is all wrong. I need answers."

With eyes like saucers, Cecile stepped back, helpless.

Drake turned back to me and his eyes burned red.

"You're the same! Just like him. What type of freaks are you?" I screamed, as I tried to maneuver from his grasp, but it was no use.

His hold on me tightened. "Give me answers, and I will release you." Drake's normal sarcastic tone had dried up and his voice became monotonous.

Realizing he wouldn't let go of me until I told him what he needed to know, I sucked in a deep breath and described my images of Cryder. Within seconds of describing every detail I could remember, someone attempted to open the door to my room, but it had been locked.

"Hello? Miss Vesten, are you alright? Why is the door locked?"

"Tell them you're fine, and I'll tell you the truth about your dreams and what's going on around you." Drake said as he slowly released his grasp on me.

"Drake, you can't tell her now. It isn't time." Cecile cried.

I stared at him while he stepped away from me, but Cecile's words rang in my ears. She knew the truth and she hadn't told me? My breath caught, and bile rose in my throat.

With a shaky voice I yelled out. "I don't know why it's locked. My friend is coming to unlock it now. I'm fine, promise." My eyes stayed glued on Drake. What could he know about my dreams? The nurse popped her head into the room, once Cecile unlocked the door.

"What's going on in here? Are you okay ma'am?" She asked wide eyed. She checked my pulse and I forced myself to relax. I needed to get answers from him.

"I...well...had a very bad nightmare. Freddy Kruger chased me, wanting to date me it was terrible." A true nightmare from my childhood ever since I saw the first Nightmare on Elm Street poster.

"She was screaming and kicking. We woke her from it." Drake continued for me.

The nurse sighed. "Do you need anything? Do I need to get the doctor?"

"No ma'am. Honest I'm fine. Just a bad dream." I needed answers from Drake.

"Alright. Be sure to buzz if you need anything. I'm Mona and I'll be your nurse until about eight." Her lips curled into a smile.

I returned it falsely. "Thank you very much."

She nodded to Drake and Cecile and then headed out the door. I could hear her fading footsteps. I glanced over at Cecile, her focus on me had quickly turned to Drake.

She shook her head slowly and stepped in front of him. "You need to calm down, seriously." She turned to me. "He can't tell you anything, Ren. Sorry, but he would be in serious trouble if he did."

"Someone needs to tell me something, now." I said through clenched teeth.

"I needed answers. It's too soon for your changing to start happening. I needed to know what you were going through." Drake stared at me still. His thin lips were set into a straight line.

He took a few steps back.

"What change?" They both ignored my questions, as though I had become invisible.

"It is too sudden." Cecile stated.

Deep in his own distant thoughts. "I bet he does not even know how far along she is. She is the one. That has to be the only explanation." Drake paced back and forth, mostly talking quietly to himself.

"So, how can it be happening so quickly? What's going on with her? You promised everything would be fine." Cecile said. The concern forced her voice to rise an octave. "This is too fast. I'm not even noticing anything yet."

My eyes traveled between them, trying to catch recognizable pieces of their conversation.

"I have only seen this once before. Our generation has been waiting for her." Drake said, continuing to pace through the room. Cecile paced behind him.

"Why are they waiting for me?" I asked.

"I doubt they are ready for her, but they need the chosen one." His mumbling continued.

"Chosen what?" He still ignored me.

"Even if she is a stubborn high school girl." He smiled then by his words, but that only pissed me off.

"Stubborn? You better not be talking about me you arrogant ass." My self-control weakened.

A smile grew on his lips and that did it. His cocky smile tore into me and ended the miniscule amount of control I still had left.

The boiling fury filled my body, and threatened to break free from my veins. His sarcasm had rubbed me the wrong way, and my body shook, along with the little table which shook in tempo with me. It rattled against the hospital wall. My anger then lifted me effortlessly off the bed. The blanket wrapped around my body shuffled to the floor and I landed weightlessly on the balls of my feet onto the tile. Any other time levitating out of bed would've scared, or shocked me, but I couldn't control any of that with anger steering my emotions.

Alarms buzzed around me when the machines connected to my body detached themselves and clattered to the ground.

I made my way to Drake,and wrapped his shirt collar in my hand. "What the hell is going on?" I growled. "Someone better answer me now! And tell me the damn truth!"

Drake stared in disbelief when I lifted all six feet of him off the ground, and tossed him across the room..

A wild fury flared inside me, and I didn't even notice the table fly slamming into the far wall beside where Drake had landed. I only saw red, and I wanted answers- badly.

Cecile backed up against the wall, and the look in her eyes held true fear. She screamed and slowly lifted her shaking hand pointing at me. "Oh m-my god! It's n-not possible. Ren, oh my god, your eyes.

"What's wrong with my eyes?" Anger bubbled inside me.

"Don't worry. It'll go away soon, right?" Her eyes skimmed over to Drake for confirmation.

"I don't know how long it lasts. Her strength is phenomenal, and her power is quite spectacular." He stood up and dusted himself off. "I didn't want to believe she was the one, but how else can you explain it? We came all this way, and he was right." He shook his head in awe.

"I don't understand. You still didn't answer about my eyes." I said.

Drake pointed to a mirror hanging above the sink in the room. I walked over to it, scared to look, keeping my face down standing in front of the flawless glass.

"You don't have to look Rena. It'll be fine. It'll clear up soon," Cecile said.

'I can do this,' I whispered and looked up. The image terrified me. A scream escaped my lips and I slammed my fists into the glass. It broke into thousands of tiny glittering pieces.

I turned my focus to Cecile, who had tears streaming down her cheeks now. "And why is it that you know so much about this? Why didn't you say anything to me? Tell me what I'm becoming?" I asked, as my bottom lip began to quiver. Tears of confusion and frustration threatened to bust through.

"Calm down Ren. Your emotions are heightened right now. Just breathe and we'll get it all squared away," Cecile said.

I ignored her and spun to face Drake. "Why did you and Cryder come here for me?"

Drake moved closer to me, finally looking me straight in the eyes. "You, my dear, are something very rare. My people, have waited for you."

"Who are your people?" I asked. "An old race. Ones that have been here since the beginning of time," Drake answered.

I heard footsteps pounding the tile headed toward my room. They sounded like herds of elephants plowing through the Savannah.

"Security," I whispered, and panicked. I couldn't be stuck here any longer.

My room sat on the bottom floor, and a window to the outside world held me in. I ran to the window, not hearing any of the words being yelled at me- or to me.   I just ran.

I raced around a corner and down the pathway to the woods behind the hospital. I wanted to escape drama, and civilization in general. I needed to think. I pushed my legs to run harder and faster until everything around me blurred. The trees and the bushes flew by me. But within seconds, the scene showed itself in high-def,and I could see an oak tree sway with the breeze as I ran past. A bush to my right held on to three limp flowers as they slowly withered by the sun, and a blue-jay splashed around in the small creek to my left.

I came to a stop, and didn't know how to feel. Fear swirled in me from my inhuman speed. The new super-power brought back the images of my red eyes and reminded me I was changing. But I had a random amount of excitement flowing out of my pores at the thought of being able to run side by side with the wind. I could also move things with my emotions or mind, or something like that, and I had Thor's super-human strength. Since I could lift up Drake without breaking a sweat.

With the red eyes, I pictured myself with Superman's laser vision. But I knew I wasn't like Thor or Superman, I had become something entirely different. A thing I had only read about, but would never in a million years have thought was real. Would I grow fangs too? Those made it obvious.

I was in the process of becoming a... as I started to admit the true answer, Cryder stepped from behind the old oak tree. His eyes. wide and bright as the moon, brought me out of my thoughts and into reality.

"Where the heck did you come from?" I asked, swatting at a fly that buzzed in front of my face.

"I'm so very sorry, Rena," he said low and quiet as the wind.

"Sorry, Cryder? Now what in the world would you be sorry for?" Sarcasm dripped from my tongue.

"Drake called me. He let me know it was time for me and you to talk."

"Well, I've been feeling a little different lately. Would you know anything about that?" I eyed him suspiciously. I waited for him to deny the truth, and I intended to toss every detail I had learned in his face.

"Yes, I do know what's causing you to be ill, however I don't believe the present time or place is appropriate for that discussion." He glanced around.

"So, when would be the best time for you, exactly? I mean its not like it's affecting me or anything." My face radiated with heat, and I had to physically keep my breaths steady until I could speak again. "I know I'm changing. I just don't know why. I also know that you're the cause of this, and I want to know why you did this to me."

"You must understand, that what's happening to you and your body is not a situation that may be stopped or controlled. The only help that can be given is guidance and reassurance, and that is what I am here for."

"Why does everyone know what's going on? Why was I left out when this obviously had something to do with me?" I said with my hands on my hips.

"Your friend, Cecile, is in the exact same predicament you are in. That's why you both bonded so strongly at such a young age. You needed each other to get through this time. There is no controlling what's destined, only allowing it to happen, and take it at its best." He glanced around again, then brought his eyes back to me. He took a step closer.

My heart played the drums against my chest and I stared into his eyes. I yearned to be with him, and didn't know where those feelings came from. I'd never felt such intense emotions for a guy I'd only just met. A tingling in my stomach had me wanting to feel his arms around me, and I had to keep reminding myself that I couldn't trust him.

I looked up at him, with all the questions flowing through my mind. I opened my mouth to ask the first question and stopped when he put his hand to my cheek. My breath caught in my throat savoring his warm hand against my skin. His palm fit perfectly against the curve of my face, and I tried to stay focused and remember what he had done to me.

"Why..." I took a deep breath, trying to feel the touch of his hand for as long as he would let me.

I had things to ask, and words to say, but having him so close suffocated me- in a good way. His woodsy scent covered me like a fog. He pulled away, dragging his hand free from my face, and turned from me.

"Rena." The deep sound of his voice sent chills along my arms. "You are changing. It is partly my fault, but the blood was in you as a child. You were destined to become like us. And we always have been destined to be together. I should have warned you before starting the bond and I am truly sorry for that."With his back facing me, his shoulders drooped and trembled, as if holding in a sob.

Goosebumps rose all over my skin, but I brought myself back to reality. His touch had pulled me away from the truth. It had made me want to be with him, and truthfully I wanted to get distance between it all. With his touch he had forced me to forget, turning me into a robot love slave like Cecile. I would be there to fulfill his needs.

"Look, I don't care what you are. I'm not becoming anything, and you need to leave now, you weirdo. Leave now before I call the cops."

He then whirled around to face me with red stained cheeks. Tears of blood dripped down his chin. "I'm sorry. I never thought this was how it would all go. A vampire, Rena. That is what I am, not some weirdo. A king. And you will be a vampire also, my queen, whether you admit to it or not."

His tears, and everything about him terrified me. My emotions ran hot and cold.

So again, I ran.

But before I got too far away, he spoke, his soft voice chiming in my ear. "We are destined you and I. It is inevitable. You will see."

Chapter 5

I stomped into the house and slammed the door behind me. Making my way to the living room, I collapsed onto the couch.

My life had changed drastically in only a few short hours, and mentally I had no idea what to think or how to feel. Physically, a power surged through me, one I've never felt before. And either my PMS was on the fritz, or the wicked witch mood swings came with being the v-word - there's no way in hell I could call myself anything other than human.

Fear was the only thing I felt around Cryder, and of course my hormones took control of the wheel too. He made me act like a typical teenager. My heart thumped louder and my breath slowed, and it all scared the living crap out of me. I haven't let anyone affect me for a long time. Simply glancing at Cryder gave me goosebumps. What did all of this mean?

"Oh, Mom and Dad, I miss y'all so much. Please help me figure this out," I whispered to their picture hanging above the fireplace. They would've had answers for me.

I needed to clear my head and get some fresh air. I slid off the couch, headed to the front foyer, and fished the keys to my fugly crap-brown Rio out of a glass bowl. The teeth of fear bit at my insides with the thought of jumping behind the wheel. After the accident I became a passenger never the driver, but the need to get out of the house outweighed it all right now.

I remembered a spot at the edge of town where my family used to sit and watch the stars. Sitting here now in silence, I felt all those good times slowly fade from my mind with thoughts about the drama that unfolded throughout the day. I had no idea what my next step would be. The ground that I stood on now shook with uneasiness dealing with vampires.

In the car on the way to my relaxing spot, my mind raced with thoughts. The books I read about sparkling vampires, and the movies I watched with how romantic people make them seem, I didn't feel that way right now. My life had crossed over into the supernatural, with me apparently being the newest member of the group, and it couldn't get any stranger. I hoped.

I made it to the cliff's edge. A spot that you could past the town of Granbury and into the beautiful hills. Lights shimmered, and stars sparkled from where I sat. I soaked it all in. Once the moon stole the sun's spot in the sky, I decided to head home.

I pulled out onto the road and came to a stop sign. I felt immediately pressed to make a decision. To go straight, meant I went home. To turn left meant to follow a path to the unknown- to the vampires.

The mansion stood tall behind the woods, and a tingle pricked the edges of my fingers wanting to flip my turn signal. Cryder could answer my questions and help me understand. But to go home meant to leave all the creepiness behind. Do I turn and face him? Or do I go straight home, and try to forget? I turned.

* * * * * * * * *

I pulled onto the street in front of the gloomy rundown mansion and all of the scary ghost stories about this place popped into my head. I shivered.

Sitting in front of their house at night, I felt like a stalker, but I needed answers and possibly wanted to catch a glimpse of the blue-eyed vampire that lived here. 'Stop thinking that way. He's dangerous.' The safe voice inside my head reminded me.

I sat in the car, not able to get out but not wanting to leave. Why am I here? He scares me. Why do I want to be in his house by myself? I decided to u-turn and escape quietly from the house, but in my rear-view mirror I caught sight of a dark shadow illuminated by street lights, creeping toward the car.

A very large steroid using pro-wrestler shape hobbled over toward me. His legs stiff as they drug across the concrete of the street. The movements were stiff like a zombie. I wanted to scream, call for help, or dial 9-1-1, but instead in a panic I slammed on the gas. My foot slipped off the pedal, and the car sputtered forward. I stepped on the pedal again ready to speed away, until a tapping on the driver side window had me slamming on the brakes, and a scream broke free from my mouth.

A muffled voice swirled to my ears. "Are you lost, sunshine?" Drake's smirk rose on his face.

His arrogance weighed on my patience immediately, but I definitely felt a small amount of gratitude that he had shown up. I would place my money on the vampire over the zombie-like dude any day.

I glanced in my rear-view mirror again, and the dark shape had disappeared. "Did you see...there was a..." What could I say? 'There was a thing walking behind my car that looked like a zombie. I mean it was completely possible for those to be real too. Yeah, that sounded sane. My newest wardrobe purchase should consist of a straight jacket.

Had Drake been behind my car? There's no way, this thing was stockier, where Drake is thin. Who had it been then?

"What are you trying to say?"

"Nothing. Sorry. Gotta go." I gave a small but pitiful smile, which probably looked more like a grimace, and started to back up again. Awkwardness filled the space between Drake and I now-well more so now.

As I slowly backed up, my foot slammed on the brakes and my heart went into over-drive. Goosebumps rose on my arms as Cryder stepped onto the porch.

He stood there in black slacks and a black snug shirt. With the sun setting behind him, he looked like an angel. His powerful gaze fixed on me. I sucked in air like it was going out of style, and tried reminding myself that breathing was a necessity. A dazzling smile brightened his face, and my heart melted into a big pile of goo. How could I even think about liking a vampire? I needed to get a hold of my sanity.

In my peripheral, Drake's smirk grew to a full blown smile like he knew of the mushiness growing inside me. He opened my car door and asked. "Shall we go in, my dear?" Without hesitating, I turned toward him, nodded, and stepped out of my car.

Each step felt like concrete filled my shoes. Stepping closer to Cryder meant getting closer to the truth, but something inside of me kept screaming that this was a bad idea. I didn't listen.

I took my first apprehensive step onto the stairs up the wrap-around porch. My heart drummed at my temples, and with each step it grew louder. I made it to the top before making eye contact with the angelic monster standing in front of me.

Cryder extended his hand for me to hold onto, and helped me through the front door. "Please come in."

Finally looking into Cryder's trusting gaze, my knees weakened. Every bad thought I had about him melted away like ice cubes on a hot summer's day.

An electric shock traveled through me by his touch, and I yanked my hand free from his. I saw a slight hint of hurt cross his face, but in the small instant it appeared it disappeared.

We took a few more steps inside, and he closed the large wooden door behind us. It shut with a loud click as the lock fell into place. I jumped.

"Head to the right. That's the living room. Have a seat." Cryder gestured with his head to the right, "I'm going to get us some drinks. I'll be right back." He walked away, and I headed to the living room, leaving the foyer that we had stepped into and admired the furniture.

Crisp brown leather filled the space, and everything looked newly purchased. I stood uncomfortably against the wall. How did you act in a vampire's house? I had expected coffins, or darkness, but they had normal furniture- from what I could tell- and their lighting was the norm as well.

The room smelled of a freshly put out fire, and it reminded me of Cryder's sweet woodsy scent. Cryder came from the kitchen with two blue water bottles, and tossed one at me.

"Thank you." I squeaked out. What was with the bottles?

He gestured with his hand for me to sit, and I did very slowly into the love seat. My legs stuck to the leather as they slid along the furniture with a ripping noise, which stood out in the uncomfortable silence.

"Please Rena, get comfortable." He collapsed into the tan recliner in the corner of the room.

I couldn't even fake being calm, apparently.

"I didn't think a place so run-down on the outside could actually look nice on the inside. This furniture is a lot comfier than it looks. I mean it looks brand new, do you not sit in it often? It's comfier than the one I have at home. Where did Drake go? Is he not coming in?" I zipped up my lips and grinned stupidly at him.

Cryder didn't treat me like a rambling idiot though, which is the way I felt. In fact he answered me. "Drake decided to give us our time to talk. He did not want to interfere but he may come in later. I like the furniture in my room better than this." He shrugged his shoulders, and sat with his arms crossed over his chest.

"Um...okay then, well get comfy here because we might be pulling an all-niter." I blushed. "I meant...I have questions that's all." I pushed the hair out of my eyes. "Anyway, let's start at, why did you do this to me?"

"The thing is Rena, as I told you before, I had begun the bonding ritual without waiting to talk to you first. I should have waited but you see I have been waiting for you all of my life. I was so overwhelmed by finding you, that I didn't want to risk the chance of losing you." He dropped his arms into his lap, and took a deep breath expanding his broad chest. His eyes fixed on mine, waiting for a response.

"All your life? How old are you exactly?" "Not the oldest, that's for sure. I'm forty-nine years old." When I didn't say anything because I didn't know what to say, he continued, "by the way, the headaches and nausea are part of the process. They are connected to the change from human to vampire."

"How did you know about the headaches?" "I have seen the bond process before. They will only worsen, until you succumb to the sacrifices required to be bonded."

My jaw dropped. How could I be expected to believe any of this? It continued to sound more and more like the fantasy novels I enjoyed reading, except right now life felt more like a horror movie instead. All this time I had wanted a handsome stranger to whisk me away, but now that it could possibly happen I felt like running away or crawling underneath my covers- curling into the fetal position and never leave.

"Um...sacrifices?"

He stared at me with his golden-blue eyes, watching my reactions. "It will end the pain. All you have to do is accept what you are, and go through a biting ritual. It really is not as bad as it sounds."

I grimaced, "well, let's just start from the beginning and go from there. I want answers, that's what I came here for." I bit into my lip to bring myself back down to earth. We're just talking, nothing else will happen. "How did you know I was your...the one?"

Oh, for heaven's sake I couldn't bring myself to say 'bond-mate'-too permanent. It sounded old-fashioned and dominating. It's my choice on who I bond with or mate with. Not that I would mate with anyone right now, not until I found that right person that I wanted to... mate with. It had to be right. My mating conversation was cut short when I heard *his* voice in my head.

You can read my thoughts, and I can read yours. I gasped.

"No I can't!" Wait...I can read thoughts? I just read his thoughts. He can read mine? Oh, dear god did he just hear my whole mating spiel? Great.

"You see? I can hear yours and you can hear mine, when I allow it." He laughed just then, a soft quiet one, it brought music to my ears. "Normally that does not work until after you have bonded with someone, however you are special my Rena. Your strengths are more powerful than expected, which means you belong to me."

I stood with sure speed the sofa moved back a couple of inches. Frustrated by his matter-of-fact tone. "Now you just listen here vamp guy. You don't own me, you never will, got it?" Fuming by his words, I thought I was blacking out because my vision started to flicker in and out. Until I saw the light bulbs flicker. That caught me off guard, and I collapsed back onto the sofa. The lights shone brightly when I took one last big deep breath. "What the hell is that? Is that me?"

Cryder chuckled and leaned forward in his chair with a gleam in his eyes like a child with a new toy. "Oh yes. That was you. Drake told me about what you did earlier and now I had a front row seat." He grinned from ear to ear. My hands were clasped over my mouth. Cryder sat still, in awe.

"What is it? What do I have?"

"That, my darling, is not an illness but a vampire given power called telekinesis. You are able to move things with your mind. When you become fully bonded no one will be able to control you or your mind. They were given to you by our ancestors, something that is already a strength of yours."

"So what's my power then? Control?"

"No, your mind is your strength. It is just remarkable. You want to know about vampires?"

I nodded, and popped the lid on the drink bottle I had been holding in my hands this whole time. When it opened a strawberry aroma filled the room. My mouth watered. "What is this, honestly? Because strawberries have never made my mouth water. Please, be honest to me."

"Ah, yes that. It may make you run away from me again, but I won't lie to you. It's a mixture of the freshest fruit grown in our community." It dawned on me then. I had been one step behind this whole time as I figured it out, it was...

"and a couple drops of my blood." His eyes moved quickly to mine and I could feel the look of horror forming on my face as the color drained out of me.

My vision went spotty and the feeling of nausea wrung itself around my stomach. I had figured out the answer, but it still didn't make me feel any better.

In a flash, Cryder sat down beside me, fanning my face and handed me the water bottle. I wanted to deny the need for the drink, but then my stomach rumbled with need. Almost instantly after taking a few sips, my stomach settled and my vision cleared. My heart rate sped up like a Lamborghini on a back road.

It wouldn't slow once I realized Cryder's arms were wrapped around me. With the closeness, I caught his scent and it filled me with contentedness. A combination of smells calmed me, but the slight hint of firewood grabbed my attention every time. It reminded me of my family and our summer camping trips. That particular smell relaxed me enough so that I could catch my breath and actually look him in the eyes.

"Are you still frightened?" He asked.

Sitting up straight, I ran my fingers through my hair. "No...yes...I don't know. That was the answer I had expected, but still hard to accept. I'm learning that most things are different with you." Concern filled his eyes. "Oh, stop looking at me like that. I said I'm not going to run away, and I meant it. But you have to give me time to soak it all in. You say this is all inevitable, and there is no way around it. And we are supposedly destined to be together and I have been drinking your blood?"

"Yes."

"I absolutely love the thought of becoming a queen. However, I am not going to jump into something so...so definite without getting to know you."

He nodded. "Let me explain from the beginning. And then maybe you can get a better understanding for our...situation."

"Yes that could help things."

"The originals, are the natural born. I am one and Drake is one. We were born by true vampire parents. You, however, are an original-made. Meaning only one of your parents was an original. All of the originals and original-made have come together and formed a community. A family, if you will, and in this family we are governed by a king. I am that king, well, the next to claim the throne at least. My strength and powers are hereditary. I can control people with my mind. I can make anyone move to where I want them to, except without truly bonding my powers are very weak. It is my birthright to become a king and to keep peace in our community. Together you and I will keep the equality as it has been done for many generations before us. To keep the secret of the vampires from humans, and to keep our rogue vampires from causing any problems. That is how it has been done, and that is how it must stay.

"For each generation, there is a queen born to sit at the throne and govern beside the king. Her powers would exceed all others but be an equal to my own. It is said that I would have to wait until my lady was at her peak, then I could start the bond.

"Their are two different rituals of bonding that must be completed. First, is a bonding tradition that you and I have begun but not yet completed. Which is the passing of my blood to you. The second, would be a ritual ceremony held on the homelands which welcomes us to the throne.

"That red juice you have been drinking is what will calm the pain and nausea. The pain, however, will worsen if the bond is not completed, as I said before. The juice, is an old family recipe, an elixir as they call it. It is for initializing the bond process, you must drink this in order to start the bond, but that is all it is good for." He took a deep breath, still so calm, and filled with a pride I had never seen in anyone before.

"Do I have to leave my friends and the life I'm use to?" That question surprised me. It sounded like I was accepting the idea of becoming a vampire-I wasn't. "I mean the powers are crazy enough, and now you are adding mind reading, drinking of the blood, and me becoming a queen to the mix. I can only handle so much, and this is a lot to take in. Also, shouldn't there be romance, flowers, and even a first date? Especially before all the craziness comes into play?" I let every thought jump from my mouth.

Cryder's pride left his face at my last statement. A crease formed between his brows with confusion. "How can you go from obvious fear of me and what I am, to undeniable acceptance? And how can you sit in front of me, not running, with the gruesome facts thrown in front of you? When it was not too long ago that you ran terrified from me. Now you sit with a straight face, talking to me, after you have learned everything."

I giggled nervously, "I want to run from you, you have no idea. But I came here to listen, to understand, and go from there. Wherever *there* might be after this. Will I be able to live the same life, and what will happen to me once I change? I have to know these answers."

His eyes, filled with compassion, stared into mine as I spoke. "We all will have to move on from this small town. Staying in one place, tends to be dangerous, especially outside of our community. You will not age as a normal human, so your appearance will stay the same. Once the bond is complete, your appetite will change. You will be able to eat normal food, but your body will require blood to survive and keep healthy. Your self-control will be...well obviously as you have seen it's already starting to be a bit out of control. It will take time to be able to grasp everything, but I will be by your side through it all. With my help and support you'll become the strong queen you are destined to be."

Right then I heard the front door creak open, and my pulse quickened. I hoped zombie guy hadn't found his way in. My thoughts skipped away from that when I heard a familiar voice followed by the most annoying giggle. My frustration with Cecile still lingered.

"Hey, did we make in time for the group sacrifice?" Drake laughed obnoxiously.

"That's enough Drake," Cryder responded.

Cecile giggled again, but stopped immediately once she saw me sitting there. "What the hell are you doing here?" I asked. "Apparently you're use to just walking into this house?"

"Yes...I've been here a couple of times." Cecile held onto Drake's hand.

"So, how many more secrets do you have? I can't even trust you any more." Anger spat from my tongue.

"She's allowed to keep secrets. She won't be able to hide them from me for long though." Drake tickled her sides.

"Drake, enough," Cryder repeated.

"What does that mean?" I asked Drake specifically.

"It means we will be swapping blood soon. Want to watch?" Drake words hit me like a brick wall.

"Enough," Cryder growled. His booming voice raised the hairs on my arms.

"What? She needs to get use to this. She's going to become one of the freaks soon. Isn't that what you called us?" A smirk formed on Drake's thin lips.

"Shut up, Drake." Cecile whined from beside him.

"Oh, you need to shut up too Cecile. Don't try to be nice now, after all the secrets you've kept. You want to change into a blood sucking fiend, go for it. I'm outta here." I stormed past Cryder without looking at him, but harshly stared at Cecile as I passed.

She started to put her hand out to grab onto mine, but I side-stepped her touch. "Don't." My only word while I marched out the door and into the normal world, wishing I had gone straight at the stop sign.

Chapter 6

I stormed down the porch, and made my way to the car. Before I could get the door opened, the crunching of dead leaves exploded behind me. In a haste to open the car door my keys fell from my hand landing with a jingle at my feet. I spun around with fists up ready to fight for my life, until Cryder's face popped into my vision. With a determined look he said,

"Rena, you mustn't leave."

"And why not? What else could you possible have to say?"

Crossing my arms, I said, "my best friend is already acting like a monster because of you both. I'm done with all of this."

"There's still a lot more for us to talk about. And even more for you to understand. It is imperative that we discuss the details."

"Well, what else is there? I can't walk in the sun or I'll sparkle in front of humans?" I laughed loudly, but inside a chill filled me. The thought of not being human terrified me.

"That is why we need to talk. There are mainstream vampires and real vampires. We are real, and there is no sparkling. You don't attack humans for their blood. It is all much different than what you think." He took a step closer.

I took a step back. "I don't care. Get it? I want to go home and live my life like I was doing before I met you."

Hurt filled his eyes, but his tone stayed neutral. "That's impossible. It can not happen."

"Excuse me? When do you get to decide what can and can't happen in my life?"

"Rena, I am not trying to push you into anything. This is your life. As a vampire and with me." He took another step closer.

I tried to step back, but I was already pressed up against the car. With each deep breath, Cryder's scent filled me. He stood so close that I felt wrapped in his sexy aroma. My fingers ached to touch his skin, and my eyes flitted shut. A wave of calm settled into my body. For the first time this week I felt relaxed. My shoulders drooped, and my breathing went back to normal.

I opened my eyes to find that Cryder had his eyes closed as well. "Did you do that?" I whispered. His eyes opened and he nodded. "How?"

"We can send emotions to each other. And once we are bonded, we will also be able to transfer images to one another." His breath tickled my nose as he spoke.

My stomach tingled and it felt like hummingbirds were rapidly beating their wings- inside of me. "Oh."

"That's all you have to say?"

"I can't think with you so close." I placed my hands on his chest to push him away, but an electricity pricked my fingertips. My fingers wanted to travel their way down his sculpted form, but I forced them to curl into fists as they fell to my sides. "There's something there between us. I can feel that, but I hate the way it's making me feel and act. You make me weak." I hated to admit it.

"You would not think that if you let your real feelings come through. You belong to me. And before you complain about how demanding I sound, this is what I know to be the truth. If you leave now, walk away and never look back, I know those headaches and all the pain you have been feeling will worsen. Only I can make the pain stop. No human doctor and no other vampire."

"What? Why will they worsen?"

"You need my blood, whether you want to accept it or not. Your body will eventually shut down without it." I cringed, "this is insane. What else is..." Before I could finish my sentence, the hair on the back of my neck stood straight up.

My head whipped around toward the woods, along with Cryder's. A cold sensation slithered up my spine. Cryder's arms went around me. I felt someone watching us from the woods.

Anger immediately warmed my blood. The anger wasn't mine, but I could feel it corrupting my emotions. Revenge against all vampires filled my thoughts, and Cryder's closeness suffocated me. I wanted to drain him of his blood and watch his tanned color fade.

A cough racked my body, ending all horrific thoughts as the need for blood rose and my throat started to burn.

A hiss flew from Cryder's mouth and he crouched protectively in front of me.

A few heartbeats later the hair on my neck settled, along with every random feeling that had overpowered me. My body collapsed back against the car, and Cryder turned to face me and pulled me into his warm body. His eyebrows furrowed with concern. "You felt all of that."

"Ugh, yeah." I shivered against his body. "W-what was that?" I rested my head on his chest.

Cryder grabbed onto my hand and pulled me toward the house. "That was someone I had truly hoped you would never have to meet, Rena." We walked through the door, and Cryder slammed it with force.

"Shouldn't you lock that?" I gestured to the door.

"He can not come in. Our house is guarded from them by ancient power." He then took me to sit on the couch.

My movements were slow. "Why is he here? What does he want? Who is he?"

Cryder picked up the blue water bottle off the coffee table, and brought it over to me. "Here drink this. It will make you feel better, I promise."

I popped the lid and the smell immediately set my taste-buds into watering mode. My stomach rumbled with want for the juice. "So, what does the guy out in the woods want?"

"Our kind has delinquents, the same as any other. We label them as rogues. Their life is based around blood. Where a regular vampire needs blood at least once a week to survive, a rogue requires it daily to live and craves it every second. They are desperate for blood and will do anything to get it."

"I felt so much rage coming from him. My thoughts had been his thoughts." I shivered. "You knew what he was thinking?"

I nodded. "I didn't know who the anger was for, but it was crazy strong." I slowly took a sip from the bottle. I hated to admit it, the juice did make me feel better.

He stared at me for a brief moment. "It The rogue's brain is wired differently, and typically only an original vampire can read or sense them."

"What does that mean about me?" I leaned back into the couch and tried to soak in what he was saying.

"I am not sure, except that you are stronger than anyone expects." He placed a hand on my knee.

I tried to keep my thoughts focused on his words, and not his touch. "Should I be worried?"

"Not at all." He grinned then. "It only shows your strength."

Looking up at him, trying to put all the pieces together, I gathered what I could of my sanity. "What's he after?"

"They are out there trying to find a moment where you are weak and unprotected Rena, so you must be strong."

"Me specifically?"

"Yes."

"Why me? You said they were after blood, and everyone has it."

"You are destined to be the queen of all vampires. Your blood is important. One single drop can give them strength. All of your blood will give a rogue back their sanity plus unimaginable powers."

My mouth dropped to the floor. "They want all of my blood?"

He nodded. "Your blood is powerful."

"You said they could regain their sanity by drinking every last drop. Were they normal once?" I swallowed another sip of elixir.

"Yes. They all had been a part of traditional vampire society. But after fifty years, if a vampire has not found their one true mate, the mental awareness scale is tipped."

"There's nothing that can bring them back from that? Well, besides my blood of course."

"No, only death brings peace. Without it, a lust for blood consumes your every action and thought."

"He had other thoughts, other needs to be met. That's what I felt in my head. I had the urge to ki..."

He cocked an eyebrow at me. "To what?"

"To kill you. He wanted me to drain you of your blood."

"Good thing you didn't follow through." He chuckled. "I had some thoughts like that floating in the back of my brain also, but my mind isn't able to controlled. My strengths are too much for some lowly rogue. But your mind is very vulnerable, and will be until you bond with me."

"How about instead we kick his ass? I'm not ready to die, Cryder, but I'm also definitely not ready to become a vampire. I want to live that's it." My mind raced with plans, thoughts, and ideas. None of which would be enough to go up against vampires.

"You cannot do a thing. This is not your fight, but it is Drake and my right to protect the ones we care about. Consider us your knight's in shining armor." His lips curled into a smile.

I rolled my eyes. "I'm not helpless. I can learn to fight, or you can teach me how to use my vampire powers. Wait did you say you care?"

Before he could answer, I heard whispers coming from upstairs. Cecile and Drake made their way downstairs, deep in conversation.

Cecile crossed the room, sat in the recliner, and locked eyes with me. A look of worry filled her them. "Drake caught me up with what's going on. He also told me what he wants from you." And then tears spilled out from the corners of her eyes.

I hopped off the couch and sat on the arm of the chair. "Cecile, don't cry. It's a lot to take in. Trust me I know, but we can figure this out."

"But it's not what I expected. I wanted to get away from my life, forget everything about my parents, but this one is scary." Her sobs grew louder as she brought her knees to her chest.

"Please stop crying. We'll get through this first, and then figure everything else out." She sniffled. "I'm sorry for acting like such a bitch earlier. I don't know what came over me." "Its them." I nodded over to the guys as they sat there staring at us.

Drake put his hands up in surrender. "Hey, we aren't doing anything to you. It's natural."

"Right, sure. Because we've always acted like drooling love sick teenagers." I responded sarcastically.

Drake smirked. "Maybe you have. How am I suppose to know?"

"Shut up, Drake. This is serious, and not some damn joke." Cecile's words shot out in a harsh whisper, but Drake got the message.

Her words sobered Drake's humor instantly, and he crossed the room in a split second. Sitting by her side, he held her in his arms. "I'm sorry love. I would never want any harm to come to you or anyone you cared about. You are mine, and I will take care of you to my last breath." He kissed her very gently on her cheek and then her lips. He slowly pulled from the kiss and turned toward Cryder. "We need to come up with something now. I will not subject her to this, especially in the weak state she is in."

Cryder lifted out of his chair effortlessly, and stared down at Drake. "What do you think I am doing? How dare you command me to do anything. Your attitude is weighing on my patience, Drake. It would be best for you to learn your position, and keep your silence your mouth." Drake bowed his head to Cryder, and they stayed like that for a few seconds. Cryder's self-control amazed me. As one of the strongest vampires, he's capable of wreaking havoc and forcing anyone to do his will, and he hasn't done any of that...yet.

I sat staring at him. Admiring his broad chest and shoulders, which were squared facing Drake. With his head held high and an unflinching gaze, Cryder's regal blood showed through for the very first time. He knew what needed to get done.

Cecile broke through my thoughts. "So is this a whole group of psycho lunatic vampire stalkers, or just one looney on his own?"

Cryder blinked his blue eyes. "As of right now there is only one. It's a possibility that there are many more around, although they don't work well in groups." He took a seat on the couch. "However, I'm sure they have figured out by now that I have found my queen, and they will want to end that." Cryder turned his gaze from Cecile to me. "You are the glue that will hold our people together and make us strong once again. "

I shuddered. I had an awful decision to make. Become a vampire and rule the race, or don't and end a whole civilization along with possibly causing my own death. "Fine then. That's even more reason for me to learn their weaknesses, and learn to fight back. Like I said, I want to live, and not be some worthless little girl hiding in a corner."

"Okay. Something sharp through the heart will put a vampire in a coma. They will only awaken when the object is removed. Fire and decapitation will kill, and guarantees no resurrections." Drake responded.

Everything I learned about vampires from every book I had read flashed through my mind. Truth and stories were jumbled together in my thoughts. "What about the sun?"

"True vampires can withstand the sun better than the rogues, their blood is weakened and not pure like ours. Sun hardens the blood creating stone from our bodies. So if you do come in contact with one, which I hope you never do, try to find the sunniest spot you can and wait there until we find you." Cecile nodded at Drake's answer, but I knew with my luck it would be a stormy day when I came face-to-face with one of them.

I sat, thinking about crosses and holy water as weapons also, but I was pulled from my thoughts by Cryder's voice.

"Rena." He called. "Rena, we are not children of some demon. We didn't rise from hell."

Great, he had heard my thoughts, again. "I didn't mean it that way."

He ignored my comment. "We are a race that was born from this world. We are in a sense, human. We do not look different, we only have different abilities. So please stop comparing the true vampire race to the blood sucking demons that you have read about in books. What we are and the blood in your veins are not related to the fiends you see on the movie screen."

"Stop reading my mind. Can I learn to block my thoughts like you do?"

"Yes." Cryder simply responded.

"Are you going to show me?"

Cryder smiled and relaxed back into the couch. "I can't teach you how to use it until you are a full-fledged vampire."

I huffed loudly. "That doesn't sound right, because as of right now my emotions and thoughts can be forced by a rogue vampire and you. I can't protect myself at all."

Cryder sat for a moment, and then nodded in agreement. "I understand. You feel helpless. I would hate to feel that way. So I would be willing to train you, but I'm not guaranteeing it will work."

"Anything you can show me, instead of running and hiding, would make me happy. As happy as I can get right now." I grinned at Cryder.

A full blown smile rose on his lips. "Well whenever you are ready my dear, I am."

Cecile yawned loudly then, and stretched out her legs. "As fun as all of that sounds, I'm done with testosterone filled tantrums, and talk about psycho vamps." She stood. "I'm ready to go pass out."

She took two steps away from the chair and fainted.

I jumped up and went to Cecile's side. Drake flipped her onto her back, and she gasped for air but her eyes remained closed.

I leaned over her, gently stroking her forehead. "Cecile? Cecile, honey can you hear me?" Cryder leaned over examining her. I asked, "what's wrong with her?"

I could feel his hot breath on my ear. "Apparently her need for blood is not being met." He glanced up at Drake and rushed to where he stood, lifting him by his collar. "If you intend to keep your mate healthy and alive I suggest you take care of her properly, and not let it get to this point ever again."

"I didn't kn-kn-know it had gone this far. I'm sorry sir. She's starting to need it daily, and there really hasn't been a schedule. I'm so-sorry."

"You know better. If she needs it daily then you know what that means, and you should be providing her better." Cryder snarled and dropped Drake back to the ground.

Drake only nodded, and then glanced down at Cecile.

"Listen, I don't give a shit who did what, someone better worry only about making my friend better. Now!" I screeched at them, and then gasped as Drake slowly brought his wrist to his mouth. "What the..."

Cryder came to my side within seconds, and whispered in my ear. "It is too late to make more elixir for her, and I'm sorry you have to see this side of us so soon. But we must take care of her now or she could die."

At those last words, the slicing sound of Drake's fangs sinking into his own flesh was all I heard at first. Then Cecile's lips wrapped around Drake's wrist. Her loud gulps filled the new silence, along with moans in between swallows as the red syrup flowed from his veins and down her throat. I sat watching as a small drip fell from her mouth and dribbling down her check, coating her pale white skin with a vibrant red.

Chapter 7

I scrunched up my nose. "Are you done yet? She looks better."

I needed to avert my eyes, the scene between the two of them felt more private than public, like watching lovers kiss. But with complete fascination I couldn't force myself to look away.

Drake blinked several times before he realized that I was talking to him. He glanced down at Cecile as she continued to slurp up the blood, a smile twisted on his normally sour puss face, and he slowly removed his wrist from her grasp.

A whine came from Cecile and reached out to Drake as a child would for their mother. She wanted his closeness, or maybe it was his blood she craved still. I couldn't accept the latter.

Cecile's body fell limp back to the floor. I rushed over and crouched beside her. "Are you okay? Feel better?"

She nodded but didn't say anything.

"Do you want help up?"

"Um, yes." She then turned to Drake. "Is it always like this? I mean drinking straight from you?"

"Yes. Straight from the source affects you a lot more." He smiled at her.

She glanced around the room slowly before returning her gaze on him. "Well, let me say I love it. That was all sorts of hot and sexy." She winked.

Drake winked back. "Oh, most definitely hot and sexy."

"Okay, okay. Get a room you two." I shook my head.

Cecile blushed. "Right, you're still here. My bad."

Drake slowly helped Cecile up, then carried her the rest

of the way over to the couch.

I stood up and felt Cryder standing silently behind me. I

turned to face him and saw him fidgeting with a splinter of

wood poking out from the wall. His fingers may have been

focused on pulling the piece out, but his eyes were glazed

over and obviously concentrating on his thoughts.

I stepped back to stand next to him. "What's wrong with

you?"

He shrugged. "Nothing."

"Whatever. Normally you're talkative, but now you're

standing back and concentrating a little too hard on the wall."

He dropped his hand, and I lowered my voice. "What's

wrong?"

He turned to look at me. "I received a phone call from

our grandfather a few minutes ago."

"And?"

He relaxed against the wall. "He knows which rogue is here."

"Who?"

"His name is Bristol. And he has a lot more than your blood on his mind. That I'm sure about."

"What do you mean?" I crossed my arms.

"I think we all need to sit down and talk. There's a lot to be discussed."

"You always say that." I huffed.

"Yes, and it's true. I can't help that."

"Fine, let's talk."

Drake and Cecile made their way over to us.

"Sorry I was eavesdropping. Heard we have to talk." Drake sighed.

Cryder gestured to the couches. "Take a seat." Once everyone sat down, Cryder took a deep breath. "When a vampire enters their fiftieth birthday, if they have not found their mate or the mate has been killed, then the deterioration phase begins. It is a very sad thing to see, especially when it happens to someone you care about. Confusion between what is right and wrong, or fact and fiction collapses around them. Their world becomes a made up land. A place that has donors, not victims. Where everyone they ever use to know have become their enemies. The world is out to get them."

"That sounds awful." Cecile nuzzled her face into Drake, and he put his arm around her.

"It is. And they are able to survive on any human blood, but they are never truly satisfied. Their bodies demand it daily. Without blood though, they will whither, die, and slowly turn to dust. Either way life without the true mate is a slow death sentence." Cryder replied.

"That is so sad. I feel sorry for them." Cecile whispered from underneath Drake's armpit.

Cryder didn't hesitate on answering. "We all feel bad for what their lives have become, but you cannot forget what they're after."

"Well what about the rogue that's after me?" I asked.

"Apparently he is an old colleague of our grandparents. My grandfather believes that he is here to take revenge on our family for killing his mate so many years ago."

"Y-your family killed his mate?" My heart raced. Was his family nothing but murderers? Am I stupid for starting to believe him?

Cryder leaned forward and kept his eyes steady on mine. "No they didn't. She had been kidnapped by another group of rogues."

"So they do work together?" I asked.

Cryder glanced at me as I sat on the recliner. "Those did. It does not happen often. This group was trying to raise the number of rogues and take over the vampires. They wanted to rule, and so they attempted to steal the children and women. My family tried to stop them, but the rogues had already disappeared."

I wrung my hands in my lap. "So his purpose is to get rid of me because he assumes your family killed his mate, and it wasn't even them? How did I get involved in this?"

"You are involved because I am the next to take the throne. My parents, the king and queen at the present time, are ready to step down. With this announcement, my blood and the next queen are connected to it. As close as I am to becoming fifty, your death will bring me to my breaking point quickly, and put the future of vampires in danger."

"Killing me, means the end of the vampires? And it w-will turn you into a rogue?" My palms grew sweaty with the realization of what making my decision could do, and why finding me and keeping me alive meant so much to Cryder.

Cryder walked over and knelt before me. His blue eyes stared into mine. "You will be fine. We will take care of you and keep you safe."

Even for a fifty year old vampire the most beautiful I had ever seen. His skin glowed healthily, and everything about him appeared young. Yet, he had lived a long life, compared to me, and the story behind those eyes peeked through when I looked into them. How could I be attracted to an old vampire guy like him? Alarms rang when I was near him, but I could feel it though. The bond he had been talking about was there. Would I admit to it out loud? No.

I stared at him, and watched the golden hue of truth filter through as I spoke. "How do we kick his ass?"

He stayed looking into my eyes briefly before turning back to the group. "My grandpa said not to aim on killing him, but capturing him and lock him up in the highly secured prison that has been around for many year to guard against problems such as this."

This time Drake spoke up. "Not kill him? What the hell?"

"Grandfather said no. We listen." Cryder snapped. "This is why we are here in the first place, Drake. You jump into things before knowing the truth. You leap when there are steps to follow and precautions to take. You definitely show your immature age when you talk like this. We can't do that any longer. There are other lives at stake besides our own. Do you understand?" Cryder snarled between gritted teeth.

He took a deep breath and continued. "The prisoners are watched over, fed, and taken care of. Our grandparents started this organization when they were only in their early teens. Their whole mission in life, at that time, seemed to work on making the world a better place for their children and grand-children."

"So, how did he escape?" No matter how scary the situation, I knew I needed to know what we were up against.

Cryder stood, walked over to the front window, and glanced out into the darkness. "My grandfather said there had been a terrible fire. Bristol was able to get out, and knew that the rule of the vampires had been past down to me. Now he is here."

Cecile wrapped her arms around Drake's waist, tears streamed down her cheeks. "How did he know that it had been passed down?"

"Every vampire can feel the change in their bones." Cryder's voice came out in a hushed tone. "I felt it before my grandfather told me."

I made my way to Cryder and stood beside him. I wrapped my hand in his, and he grinned as he intertwined his fingers with mine. A heat-wave crashed into my body instantly and sweat formed on my forehead. His touch created strong reactions from me, and I didn't know why. The only thing that made any sense was that we're meant for each other. No one's touch had ever impacted me as much as his does, and I felt determined to never let it go.

"Well, what do we do from here?" Cecile shakily asked.

"Yeah, what happens now?" I asked, and put my fists up. "Do we fight?"

Cecile giggled silently, which in turn put a grin on my face.

Cryder didn't seem amused. "I wish you two would take this seriously."

I turned to him. "A sense of humor comes in handy sometimes, get one."

"Not here and not now. Drake and I will take care of that part. I want you to know exactly what you are up against." Cryder responded.

"Listen, I already told you I'm ready. So teach me. Got it?" My heart raced from frustration. How could I not be taking this seriously? "You will not tell me how I'm suppose to react, and you better not expect me to hide in the corner. I will be damned if I'm going to just sit this one out. So you will teach me, and will not treat me like a child ever again. Understand?" I held my gaze, not blinking once, with Cryder.

I watched his eyes, as many different emotions swirled through them. "You are right. You do need to be trained in case we are ever caught off guard. However, Bristol is a pure-blood, and you are no match for his strength."

I let out a whoosh of breath that I didn't know I had been holding.

He reached down and grabbed my hand, slowly bringing it to his lips. Goosebumps ran from my toes to the top of my head. Flames of desire flicked at my stomach, and I wanted those sweet lips to travel all over my skin. And for Cryder to show me how strong his need for me really was.

"First off, Rena," Cryder's words halted my wandering thoughts. "You must learn to block those thoughts," he said with a smirk on his face.

Did he hear my thoughts again? I yanked my arm away and turned. I knew my face had become the brightest shade of red known to man. "Yes, I think that's a great idea," I mumbled.

"We also need to get you comfortable with your senses. To hear and smell at a distance is something vampires are great at, and it often comes in handy," Cryder said to everyone.

My hearing and sense of smell already had grown. I had figured that out when I was running through the woods. Even now the smell of rain in the distance clung to my nostrils through closed windows, and I could hear the cries of a lone wolf in the woods. My mind categorized every sound and scent like a book shelf.

Cryder watched me as I listened to all the different sounds of the night. "You don't have a problem with that do you Rena?"

I shook my head.

"What? Really?" Drake sounded shocked.

"Let's try to test this out, okay?" Cryder asked me.

I gave a half shrug, not completely in the mood to be a test subject.

"Alright then Drake, let's start the test."

Drake nodded, stood up, and meandered out of the room. I heard his footsteps treading lightly on the wooden floor, and enter through a creaking door. By listening to the sound reverberating through the house, I could tell that he had made his way to the kitchen. Opening the refrigerator with a click, and then he pulled a plastic container out. I couldn't quite figure out what was in it, until he popped the lid. A rich smell of pure perfection slammed into me.

"Rena, can you tell me where Drake is?" Cryder had taken a seat on the couch. He and Cecile watched me.

"He w-went to the kitchen," I answered trying to control my urge to fly into the kitchen and drain the blood from the plastic bottle in Drake's hand.

"Okay. What did he do in the kitchen?"

I breathed deeply. "He pulled out a bottle filled with blood." I looked at Cryder. "Your blood."

Cryder nodded with a grin forming on his lips.

"Holy crap Rena! That's impressive. I couldn't do that right now, there are way too many sounds around this house. I can't concentrate on just one." Cecile smiled at me.

Cryder only stared at me as Drake came around the corner with the bottle still in his hands. He tossed it to me with the lid still opened. When I caught the bottle liquid spilled onto my hand and the floor, and my stomach rumbled almost instantly. Did I crave the blood?

"Let's try to send emotions to our mates..." Cryder stopped as he saw my wince at the word-mates. "Okay then, partner, we want to share emotions with our partner." He corrected himself. "You and your *partner* should be able to share. This will be a helpful thing if you are ever to be separated from each other. You will be able to sense when the other is in danger, scared, in pain, or even happy."

"You can do that without touching?" asked Cecile.

"Yes. It takes a lot of practice and a true bond between partners." Cryder kept his eyes on me the whole time, and I could feel my face flush.

Drake and Cecile sat on the couch together. "Can we try with touch first?" She smiled.

"Absolutely. Anything that involves touching you sounds great." Drake winked.

Cecile wiped her hands on her pants and then placed them into Drake's open palms. She had a constipated look as she scrunched her nose trying to concentrate.

Cryder and I watched the two of them as they focused on sending emotions.

"That was great Cecile. I felt something creep into my mind. " Drake smiled.

Cecile huffed from exhaustion. "I tried."

"How about you give it a try now, Rena," Cryder said as he found an open spot on the floor.

I sat in front of him and scooted forward so I could place my hands in his. His sparkling blue eyes stared into mine, and I tried to slow my breaths that naturally sped up by his touch.

"Okay well here goes," I announced and closed my eyes.

My mind immediately began swimming with thoughts. I sloshed through them and tried to find one that would fill me with emotions. I felt my eyes squishing together and forming the constipated look, until I found a memory that instantaneously brought strong feelings to the front of the line.

The image of my parents became the only thing I could see. Their smiling faces and the way they leaned into each other brought hot tears streaming down my cheeks. The salty flavor rushed onto my lips and my voice shook. "Did you want to try it without touching?"

"Your parents are beautiful," Cryder responded as he squeezed my hands.

My eyes shot open. "You saw them?"

He nodded.

"Hey, you could see into her mind?" asked Cecile.

"Yes. I saw inside. Your mind is filled with so much...grief." Cryder's eyes were rimmed with red.

Was he sad for me?

"A few things I still have to get over," I commented nonchalantly, and let go of his hands.

The wall between us appeared to be slowly breaking down, and it continued to scare me. I could feel myself falling for him, but I wasn't one hundred percent on the vampire band wagon.

"Are you alright?" Cryder still eyed me as I sat in front of him, hugging my knees to my chest.

"Um, yeah. I guess," I answered. "Why could you see that?"

He shrugged. "Honestly, I can only give you the same answer I've been giving you."

"That I'm screwed up? An anomaly?" I questioned back as I hugged my knees even tighter against my chest.

Cryder came over to where I sat, and placed his hands on each side of my face. "No," he replied sternly. Then his whole demeanor softened as he said, "you are becoming the true queen."

Chapter 8

Cecile and I decided to forget the training for the night. We also decided, for safety reasons only, to spend the night in the guy's house. And I laid in one of the beds of a spare room in the mansion without being able to sleep as Cryder's words played over and over in my mind. How could I be gaining vampire queen powers, when I wasn't even a full-fledged vampire? What would be expected of me? I glanced over at the clock on the night stand next to my bed and realized it was well past midnight. I didn't feel like sleeping, but I knew I needed to get some rest. My eyes may not have been ready for sleep, but my body was worn out. Would night become my day soon? Once my eyes started to close, a knock on the bedroom door forced them to open. I climbed out of bed, wrapped the black robe that hung on the outside of the closet door around my body, and went to open the door. On the other side stood a fully awake Cryder.

"Hey."

"Um, hi."

"I've been downstairs trying to read, but the way tonight ended bothered me. I wanted to apologize."

"For what?" I asked as I opened the door wider and gestured for him to come in.

He immediately went to sit on my bed. "All the info I've been throwing at you. And rushing you into becoming queen. I'm sure it's all frightening." His eyes held true concern.

I headed to sit on the opposite side of the bed. "Yes, it's a lot to take in. I feel like I'm living on the set of a scary movie, because there is now way this can be real. But everything you have told me so far has panned out, and I find myself safer around you than I ever have on my own. And then my mind remembers everything I have been through in the past weeks, and the thought of what you really are and what you want from me, I get scared all over again."

"I understand Rena, I really do. Deciding to become a vampire would be terrifying for anyone. It's glamorous in the movies when you think it won't ever really happen, but now that you are faced with it I know it's tough to accept. But I'm here. I want to make the transition less frightening for you. I don't want you to hate me when it's all over with."

I took a deep breath. "Deep down, I know you do. I can almost sense it. It's like I can tell that you're telling the truth. But I'm having a hard time listening to my gut and not my mind warning me to run away from you."

"One day maybe you'll see it, and know that you're gut is what you should be listening to. I am willing to wait for that day." He scooted about an inch closer to me.

My breath caught in my throat. "Well, um, there's one thing I've been meaning to ask. How did I get the vampire blood mixed in with my human blood?"

"Your grandparents came from a long line of vampire royalty. Another set of vampires governed by your family. There are groups all over the country. Only one king and queen, but you and I were in a sense betrothed by our parents. Your mom wanted what was best for you, but she had wanted to wait until you were eighteen, to understand the reasons why she did what she did. We waited too long. " His tone softened. "I really am sorry about the accident, Rena."

I took a few breaths. "Thank you. So I'm sure your people were thrilled to find me."

"We were. You gave me a future and the rest of the vampires. As I said before, you are the glue."

I groaned. "Don't say that."

"Why? It is the truth."

"Yeah, but that's just added pressure that I don't need right now. Okay?"

He shrugged. "Okay. I promise not to say it again. Do you accept my original apology?"

"Of course. I'm done with being so dang angry." He closed the distance between us, and I playfully smacked his leg. The second my hand touched him, that same strong jolt climbed up my arm and ran all over my body.

My breathing stopped as Cryder took the hand on his leg and brought it to his lips. His soft mouth pressed against my skin and golf-ball sized goosebumps popped up all over. He then lifted my arm and wrapped it around his neck, and my hand instantly found his hair.

His breathing had increased and it tickled my nose as he bent his face closer to mine. His tender lips brushed against my cheek. My stomach somersaulted by his touch, and it sent sensations all over my body. His lips moved toward mine when my brain screamed at me.

Stop! You need to stop.

I jerked back before Cryder's lips found mine, and place a hand on his chest. "I can't," I said huskily as I tried to catch my breath.

"Why? What happened?"

I stood up and took a few steps away from the bed. "I don't know. I just can't do this." I shook my head. "I mean I can. I really really can, but shouldn't."

He started to stand up.

"Stop. Don't move," I commanded with force behind my voice.

Cryder stayed in his sitting position, staring at me, and not moving. His lips curled to one side. "Very...interesting."

"What?"

He tried to stand up again, but his movements were slow. He strained to straighten his body as if a force tried to hold him down.

"What's wrong with you?" I asked taking a step closer.

He smiled. "This...is...all...you." His words slowly slipped from his lips.

"What do you mean me?"

"Your...mind...is...holding me."

"Cryder, what the hell are you talking about? Just act normal."

With those words, he stumbled a few steps forward, and stretched his arms above his head.

I didn't know what he was talking about. "What happened?"

"You happened, my love. Your powers keep growing." The corners of his eyes wrinkled by his huge smile.

My mouth dropped. "How did I...What did I?"

"Your mind is a powerful thing. You didn't want me to stand, you wanted me to stay in place, and so your mind built something similar to a force field around me. Any mere human, or less powerful vampire would be basically stuck there until you commanded them to do otherwise." His eyes glowed in the dim lighting, filled with giddiness.

I started to walk toward him, but stopped dead in my tracks when one of his thoughts slipped through a crack from his mind block.

She is the chosen one. I need her.

My mind was right. "That's it isn't it? I feel a connection through our touch, thinking there is some deeper meaning, but it's probably just something you are doing to make me feel that way."

"What are you..."

I interrupted his question. "Don't. I heard your thought. All you want is the queen, someone to fulfill your prophecy. All you want is the power. I'm tired of being that stupid teenager. I'm done with this shit." With those words I stormed out of the room, not waiting to hear anything he had to say.

I walked over to Cecile's room, expecting to find Drake with her, but she had been asleep.

She opened the door rubbing her eyes. "What?" she asked in a raspy voice.

"I'm leaving," I said.

She finally looked straight at me and I'm sure she caught sight of my red face. "Rena, what happened?"

"I'm tired of being a puppet following on these guys every whim. I thought Cryder and I had something or it was starting, but I was dead wrong. So do you want to come with me?"

"But isn't that creepy vamp guy out there now?"

I rolled my eyes. "We're just driving. No big. I just know I need to get out of here."

She stared at me. "I-don't-know-Ren. That makes me...nervous."

"Fine I'll go by myself."

She sighed loudly. "No. Fine. God you are crazy and seriously scaring me."

"I'll wait for you downstairs." I walked off ignoring every other comment besides the one I wanted to hear, and headed downstairs.

As I made it to the foyer, Cryder's footsteps pounded the floor as he made his way to me. I crossed my arms as he stood at the bottom of the steps watching me.

"It isn't safe out there." He said.

"Probably safer out there than here. With people that claim they are looking out for our own well-being, but instead it's for their own benefit." I stopped his words again as I lifted my hand up, open palm facing him. "Or how about making us think we are falling for you, or vice versa, only to find out yet again it's for personal gain. Thank you for making me feel foolish, but I'm done with it."

Cryder started to say something, but was interrupted again by a pleading coming from Drake.

"Please don't go. It's dangerous out there," he begged.

"I'm sorry, but Rena needs me. If she's not comfortable being here, I won't let her leave alone. I'll try to calm her down, then we'll come back. Okay?" Cecile reassured him.

I heard a loud sigh, assuming it came from Drake. "But Bristol is out there. He wants to kill you. Do you not understand that?"

"We're just going straight home. That's it."

They made their way down the stairs.

Drake protested again. "Your house isn't protected like ours is. He can walk in whenever he wants to."

This time Cecile sighed dramatically. "It's one night Drake. Chill out. We'll be fine."

She finally stomped away, stepping around Cryder, and made her way to me.

Cryder stepped forward. "Rena, don't go. It's imperative that you stay. For your safety."

"And for your people right? That's it. That's what I'm good for." I responded. I knew it was unsafe outdoors unarmed and untrained, but I couldn't stand being in this house any longer. His words swam circles around my brain, reminding me that I'm needed on a whole other level than just plain-old love. I knew it also seemed selfish of me, or stupid, but I needed to breathe. It felt like the walls were closing in around us and soon they would topple on top of us and we wouldn't have a chance to escape if we didn't try now.

"You ready?" I asked Cecile.

"Rena, I demand that you stay." Cryder growled.

"Excuse me? Demand? Who do you think you are? You may be a king of fairy land but you aren't mine," I spat back.

He stepped in front of my path to the front door. "I can't let you leave."

"Can't? Or won't? It doesn't matter. I can control this. Move." This time *I* demanded.

Cryder froze in his spot, and Drake came to his side. "You stupid fool. All he's done is take care of you and this is how you treat him?"

"Watch your words Drake. I'm in a pissy mood. All I want is to leave," I said.

"You ca..."

"Drake. Stop. Just leave it alone. She needs this." Cecile cut him off.

"Let's go," I said to Cecile. Then to Cryder I commanded, "act normal."

I turned toward the guys. "Thanks for the hospitality." With that I opened the front door, waited for Cecile to follow, and slammed it behind us.

As we backed out of the drive-way, Cryder sprinted to my window with vampire speed. "Rena, you're gaining control of your powers, but you aren't in full control. Come back inside, let's really train and let me explain."

I didn't roll down my window. "You always need damn time to explain, Cryder. But I'm tired of listening. I thought it all finally made sense, but I was wrong."

I wanted to get away from him. Every time I glanced into those blue eyes my heart did flips and my mind was filled with him. I couldn't concentrate on anything else but him, and I enjoyed having a mind of my own. I sped off, away from him, and watched those sparkling blues disappear in the rear-view mirror.

"Rena, sweetheart, please slow down." Cecile's words broke through my thoughts. "I know you're upset, but I don't think curves are suppose to be taken this fast," Cecile said while holding the oh-shit-handle with a death grip.

I looked down and realized I was going eighty-five, so I took my foot off the gas. "Sorry. I wasn't paying attention."

"It's fine. I understand. They're both just so...extreme."

"He makes me insane, Cecile. I have never let someone affect me this way, and when I finally do it ends up being one-sided." I slammed my hands onto the steering wheel so hard it stung.

"I don't think I have ever seen you get so worked up over some guy."

"But he's not just some guy, is he? He gets under my damn skin and yet I have feelings for him. Ugh, you know what never mind. I never talked about this alright?"

"Sure, no problem," she agreed.

There were nothing but back roads on the way to the house. And once it hit me that I was the one behind the wheel, the queasy feeling fell into the pit of my stomach. I needed to calm down before I had a panic attack.

Darkness surrounded us as I drove. Streetlights were non-existent and trees folded over us like we were traveling into another world. A strange feeling seeped into my skin and tightened around my bones.

Less than a mile to go before we made it to town, my car swerved and a slapping noise against the pavement bombarded the silence.

I stepped on the brakes and pulled it slowly to the side of the road. Getting out of the car, we found the front passenger tire had gone flat.

"Great, exactly what we needed out in the middle of effing nowhere. What are we going to do now?" Cecile asked.

The hair on the back of my neck stood straight up and the unnerving feeling inside of me thickened. My hands shook. "I-I don't know. I don't know how to change a tire. Do you?"

She shook her head. "Let's call Drake or Cryder to come and help us. I don't feel like standing out here in the middle of nowhere central. It's freaky."

"The last people I want to talk to right now."

"Who else can we call? Think Rena. We're out in the middle of nowhere with a flat." She turned from me and mumbled, "I knew I should've stayed at their house."

"Shut up. Okay? I was wrong, but now is not the time to shove it in my face. I'll just grab my phone and you can try them." I reached into the car and pulled my phone out. "Of course this would happen," I said through gritted teeth.

Cecile ran over to me. "What is it?"

"No signal. There's never a signal when you need it the most. Do you have your phone?"

She shook her head. "In my haste in following your outrageous plan, I left my phone charging. What are we going to do now?"

"Well, I have free towing service." Cecile's eyes went wide with excitement, until I burst her bubble. "But I have to be able to call out."

"Oh. Right. Can't you send your emotions or whatever out to Cryder? You were really good at that."

I shook my head and laughed humorlessly. "Relying on vampire powers now. Great." I sighed loudly. "Okay, I guess I can try that." I closed my eyes letting my fear and frustration fly from me, hoping it worked as strongly as it had earlier.

"I hope that worked, 'cause I don't want to have to walk."

I made my way over to the driver's side to get in, and Cecile got in on her side. We sat, not talking for a few moments.

Then Cecile turned to me and broke the silence. "Rena, I think you should give Cryder a chance."

I rolled my eyes. "Not this again."

"I know. I know. You don't want to talk about it, but you need to look into it a little deeper. What are your senses telling you about him?"

I looked down, soaking her words in, but to accept and go along with it wasn't me. "If only I knew that he cared, at least a little, and it isn't all about dedication to his clan. I couldn't handle being duped into falling for him, changing into a vampire, and then the rest of my life being stuck in hell."

"What do you think will happen if you don't accept the change? Cryder said the pains will worsen and we will die."

"I don't know what'll happen, Cecile. But those are his words, doesn't mean it's the truth."

"Do you not feel that it's the truth?"

"I don't know. What do you think?"

"I think his words are true. I can feel that. I always have, but it's stronger now. He cares for you. He loves you, but doesn't want to scare you by showing it too much."

"How did you get all of this?"

"I think it's my power. Reading people. Pretty cool huh? Drake and I had tried it out. Every day he has been making me guess what he's feeling, and every time I guessed right. Anyway, honestly you should trust in Cryder."

"But I don't want to be his follower. Because he says or demands something, that's the way it should be."

"Well, it's not like you have all the time in the world to sit on this decision either."

"I have six months. I know that. Six whole freaking months to decide if I want to be a vampire queen for all of eternity."

Cecile opened her mouth to say something, but I shushed her. A rustling sound right outside the car caught my attention.

Barely able to hear myself over my own heartbeat, I whispered, "did you hear that?"

Cecile nodded and started to reach for the handle of the door, and I yanked her back. "What are you doing?"

"It's probably the guys." She reached for the handle again.

"Stop," I whispered. "I'm not getting a good feeling about this."

My words were too late as Cecile stepped out of the car. I climbed out from my side and went to pull her back inside.

On the surface I hoped and prayed that it was the guys snapping the twigs in the woods in front of us, but my body screamed at me to climb back in the car or run as fast as I could. The thing on the other side of the bushes was not a friend of ours.

Cecile started to open her mouth to say something, but I put my hand over it and shook my head. I gestured toward the car, and she nodded in response.

We turned and started to rush to get back in the car, but not fast enough. *It* ran with vampire speed, and lifted Cecile and I off the ground by our throats. Squeezing tight enough to control our breathing, but loose enough to not completely cut off our circulation.

My feet weren't even close to touching the ground anymore, and my heart pounded out a bass solo. I could hear Cecile breathing loudly next to me.

"Mmmmm, half-lings. My favorite desert after a big dinner." His deep voice slithered out of the darkness like a snake.

He released the grip on our necks, and we collapsed to the ground gasping for air. I grabbed onto Cecile, but before we could even stand the monster was able to get in front of us and block our path.

He had a gleam in his eyes as they glided over my frame from head to toe.

He was terrifying to look at.

In the place where his eyes should have been, he had sunken-in empty black holes. He tripled my height and weight. His body bulged with muscles from his neck and down to his tree trunk thighs. He was covered in dirt and grass stains, but underneath that he had on frayed jeans and a t-shirt that constricted around his torso by mere threads.

He took a step closer, and we took a step back.

The vampire bowed his head. "My queen. Do not be frightened. It's a pleasure to make your acquaintance. I hoped I would run into you."

How did he know about me? His words stunned me into silence.

He lifted his eyes as he spoke, "I assumed I would've had to wait patiently for you, but it appears you have fallen right into my lap. The gods are watching over me."

I couldn't keep my eyes off of him. One- He terrified me. Two- I knew if I looked away I would be dead in seconds.

Cecile stood beside me shaking, with her hand in mine. I gave her a reassuring squeeze, and attempted to keep my unsteady legs from collapsing.

The monster stood straight and stared into my eyes, and a smile formed on his lips. "How wonderful that I would get to drain you so soon, and you brought a treat with you."

My eyes felt like they were about to pop out of my head. How did he know who or what I was to become? Could he smell it on me?

Cecile swallowed audibly, "w-who are y-y-you?"

His fangs slid down from his gums.

This vampire was the rogue we had heard about. A vampire so filled with rage and the overwhelming need for blood. My blood would be his greatest reward. Without a queen to help lead, the vampire race would become extinct. Revenge would be made, and he would gain great powers.

"So, you're Bristol," I said. My fear sat on the surface, but I tried to talk and act calmly. No sudden movements.

He kept his gaze back on me showing his fangs as he smiled, and his soulless eyes watched like a hawk. "How rude of me to not introduce myself. My queen, Rena, you are correct. I am Bristol."

Chapter 9

This couldn't be happening right now. The one vampire I had been warned against, now stood a foot in front of me. All the focus I had put into trying to be strong began to drain from me, and I felt my legs growing weaker the longer I stood on them. I felt my lungs closing. I couldn't breath or move. I prayed now that my emotions had made their way to Cryder, he would be our only way out of this.

"Rena is that look of shock on your face for me? How wonderful." Bristol practically squealed in delight. "Apparently you have heard of me before?"

"You don't hide very well," I responded.

Bristol pouted. "I would've preferred to have some surprise with our first meeting. But that look on your face and the smell of fear sweating out of your pores helps. Remember that feeling my face brings as I drain every drop of your precious blood. I'll let the friend watch for kicks."

I snarled, "you sick bastard. Whatever you have planned leave her out of this."

Bristol smiled like a kid at Christmas. "Oh, a feisty one. I can feel that power sizzling underneath your skin. I'm glad you haven't changed, you'll taste a hell of a lot sweeter with that human blood floating around." He licked his lips, and took a step closer. "Now relax. I'll try my best to be as gentle as I can."

"Shut up. Just let her go, this is between you and me." I stood protectively in front of a trembling Cecile.

"Your protectiveness is pointless but cute. In the end you both will die." The smile seemed glued on his face.

I rolled my eyes. "Whatever. If you're here to kill then do it already and stop bullshitting." I scrunched up my nose. "I can smell you rotting from here."

"Ren, stop." Cecile's voice squeaked out.

"You should listen to your friend. It doesn't help to make me angry," he said.

I could feel sweat building on my forehead, and hoped like hell that he would keep talking and give us some extra time to come up with something. I needed a plan, or a hope that the guys were on their way. My fear sat inside of me, and I tried my hardest to push it away.

Any time the tingle of fear would trickle up I forced myself to stand taller. Like mom always told me, 'when you're afraid, or if you feel intimidated, lift your chin and stand tall don't let them see it. Show them you are proud of who you are and nothing less.' Now I knew why she pushed for me to be stronger than everyone else, because she had to fight her whole life with her own differences. She knew I would change and would have to go through the same things. All of the tough parenting was so I wouldn't be afraid or over-whelmed by what I would eventually become. To accept the vampire blood in my veins, and to learn to take control of it. Remembering her words brought on a new understanding- I am half vampire destined to become the queen and there is no changing that.

Bristol reached out toward Cecile's trembling body behind me with extra fast vampire speed. That brought me back to reality and out of my thoughts. He was going to kill us if I didn't do something now.

"Stop!" I screamed.

Cecile shrieked and put her hands in front of her face waiting to be manhandled by the over-sized vampire, but the sound of her yelling faded out as she realized that Bristol *had* stopped.

He froze halfway to Cecile's throat, and a sneer had formed on his lips as he glared at me. He stood frozen to the spot.

"Oh my god. Ren what happened?" Cecile whispered.

"Part of my powers. Come on we have to get out of here before he breaks free." I grabbed onto Cecile's arm and yanked.

She followed me, but kept her eyes glued on Bristol. "Can he get out of that?"

I shook my head. "He will eventually but if it's anything like Cryder, it'll take a while."

"You did this to Cryder too?"

"Not on purpose."

We moved far away enough into the trees and bushes that Bristol's frozen body was hidden from our sight, and hopefully we were hidden from his.

"Where are we going? Why are we going toward the woods?"

"We need to get away. Away from..." Rustling sounds in the woods stopped us from taking any other steps.

"W-what is th-that?" asked Cecile.

"Shh. Don't let him know we're here," Cryder whispered from behind a bush. "How did you get away?" he asked as he stepped out of the bushes.

"Um. Well, my voice." I shrugged.

"Oh you did it again?" Cryder amusingly asked.

Sarcasm filled me. "Yes. The anomaly strikes again."

"You were amazing, Ren. You saved us," Cecile said with a shaky voice.

"Are you alright?" Drake stepped from behind a tree and wrapped his arms around Cecile. She nodded.

Cryder wrapped an arm around my shoulders, and glanced around the trees. "He's starting to move. Please go and sit in the car. Wait for us to come and get you." We both nodded and walked toward the car. We had gone in quite a ways into the woods, and took the long way back to the car.

Bristol broke free from my hold with a ferocious growl which echoed through the woods. The fight between the guys started immediately. I glanced toward where they were. I caught a blur of movements. All that could be heard were grunts, snapping of twigs and dry leaves, along with whooshes of air as they slammed through the forest.

Bristol's body slapped against the tree and maniacal laughter filled the woods. "Your queen bitch over there had more force in her than you two put together, and that was with her eyes closed."

"Shut your damn mouth," Cryder hissed.

"She has such great power. I can smell her sweetness from here," Bristol said as he licked his lips.

He started to stand, but Cryder stepped in front of him and planted a foot into his throat. "You won't go anywhere near her. If you even think about it you son-of-a-bitch. I will kill you," Cryder growled. "I should kill you now."

"Like you could kill me, king. Even I know you're not in full power," Bristol choked out, then he raised his hands in surrender. "I'll leave...for now, but..."

Cryder cut him off. "Go now," he snarled. "I may not be in full power but you have two royal pure-blood vampires standing over you, which means you have no chance. Run now like the pansy-ass you are, or we'll tear you limb for limb."

"Whatever. Fine. I said I would go," Bristol choked. "But trust me, your majesty, you will see me again."

"Counting on it." Cryder took his foot off of Bristol's throat.

Bristol staggered to a standing position, and his eyes found mine. He winked.

Cryder and Drake took there spots blocking us from his view, but I was able to peek through a hole between the guys. Bristol bowed to them and then with blurring speed fled from the forest.

* * * * * * * *

As soon as we walked in to the house, Cecile and I went straight for the couch and collapsed. Cryder and Drake followed locking the door behind them, both with straight lines for lips.

"Why didn't you kill him? I mean he was going to kill us with no problem," I said.

"By my Grandfather's order we don't have a right to kill, only to capture. But here we don't even have the means to hold him securely," Cryder responded.

I rolled my eyes.

"Where are we to keep him? In the house that is protected to keep rogues like him out?" Cryder asked with a hint of sarcasm sticking to his words.

"Fine, Cryder. I understand. You have to follow rules, but do you really think he's gone?" I questioned.

"No. But we will be ready the next time," he said through gritted teeth. "What happened tonight was the exact reason why we asked you two to stay with us. It's too dangerous for you to be alone. Whether you like it or not, we will be around at all times," Cryder spoke sternly.

I nodded without any protest, and was too exhausted to put up a fight. He had been right all along.

Cecile and I agreed to stay with the guys.

Drake and Cecile cuddled up with each other on the couch, and had been whispering and giggling. They stood at the same time making their way to the entry way staring into each others' eyes. Then Cecile faked a loud obnoxious yawn. "I am exhausted. I think I need to go rest, and relax. Maybe find something to relax me." She looked at Drake and winked the most exaggerated wink- she honestly didn't know how to be subtle. Drake stayed on Cecile's heels as they made their way upstairs, and stumble through his bedroom door. After their staged exit, and the click of the door being locked, my pulse picked up speed. We were alone.

Before there could be any awkward silence, Cryder stood up and headed to the kitchen. When he came back into the room he held a water bottle filled with the elixir he had been giving me for the past weeks.

My mind yelled at me not to drink it, but the second I twisted the lid off the bottle my mouth watered like clockwork. My body craved the sweet yet tart liquid in the bottle. I took a long slow swig of the delicious fruity red drink, and accepted the truth this time. Cryder's blood was sliding down my throat and filling my body. His life's source offered energy, and a way to live.

"So Cryder," his named flowed flawlessly off of my tongue, and I calmed myself before I continued. "Since we're down here together, I do have a few more questions that I'd like to know the answers to. I want to know more about what fate has in store."

He smiled which showed his beautiful white teeth and made his gorgeous blue eyes sparkle as he spoke to me. "Well, alright Rena," the sound of my name passing through his lips sent a shiver down my spine. "I will answer your questions."

My self control faltered slightly by his pearly whites. He had been standing in front of me as he spoke, and only now as I returned his smile with my own, did he come and sit next to me on the love seat. His gaze locked on to my eyes, and I never wanted to look away. I took a deep breath and asked huskily, "I know that our fates are sealed and I am destined to be a vampire. I also know I'm supposed to be a queen, but how can I rule a race that has been roaming earth for millions of years and yet I've only been alive for sixteen? Plus I don't know anything about vampires, how can I comfort and console the people that will be looking up to me, when I don't know them or what they believe in?"

He placed a hand on my knee. "These notions will all come back to you when you are truly awake, after you have changed, and we go through the vampire rites ceremony. Once we have taken our rightful place at the throne, you will begin to see the vampire world for what it is and how it needs to be taken care of."

I nodded. "Will the changing part hurt? What about you biting me, will that hurt?"

"To be honest, when I bite you there will be some pain but if you don't tense up the pain will turn to pleasure. When it comes to the change, your body dies, and reforms itself to fit your new lifestyle." I cringed at the thought. "I know it sounds awful, but when you wake up you will remember only bits and pieces. Your organs will stop working. The digestive system and all other sub organs will then reconstruct to your new more powerful body. You will still have a beating heart, blood in your veins, and a flush in your cheeks."

I sat and stared for a moment. "What about the need for blood?"

"The necessity for blood will lessen after the change as well."

I opened my mouth to ask another question, but stopped when a scream vibrated through the walls of the house. "That was Cecile!" I yelled. I ran upstairs.

A loud thud brought me to a skidding stop, but Cryder kept going to the top of the steps and only slowed when he made it to Drake's door.

I took a deep breath not realizing I had been holding it. Before I could see what happened, Cryder let a growl escape his lips and pounded the door, tackling Drake to the floor. I heard the guys shouting obscenities at each other, but I couldn't make out the words. The only sound that stood out was the beating of my heart and soft whimpers coming from the body laid out on the floor. It was *her* body. Cecile had her eyes closed, and blood pooled around her head.

I screamed until I ran out of air, and collapsed next to her. Dragging her limp body toward me, and laying her head into my lap. Blood soaked through my clothes as I held her. Hot tears streamed down my cheeks silently.

I stared up at the two guys. Cryder now had Drake pinned against the wall, but his gaze stayed on me.

"Help me. Help me please. There's so much blood, I don't know how to fix her," I whispered. I turned my eyes on Drake, and my anger flared. "What've you done? You bastard. What've you done?"

My anger boiled, and all I wanted was Drake dead for what he had done. The dressers in the room began to shake. The mirrors rattled, and I knew my powers waited now to be used. All I could see was red. Drake's life would end tonight. I pictured everything in my head. The way the furniture would crush Drake, and how his life would be taken. That all faded when I heard a whine come from Cecile.

A touch of her hand on my arm finally broke the spell of anger, and I looked down into her face. But when I stared down at her another scream bubbled in my throat. Large pointed fangs poked into her lower lip, and bright red eyes burned holes into mine. She was a vampire.

The scream I had tried to stifle exploded free. I clasped my hands to my mouth. I crawled backwards and away from Cecile. Her eyes stayed on mine. Her breath came out slowly. I collapsed to the ground in a heap, trembling like I had just been electrocuted by some unseen force. I couldn't control my body. Tears streamed down my cheeks and dripped from my chin to the floor in little puddles. With every move I made, Cecile's breathing sped up. I wrapped my arms around myself and felt a shiver thread itself inside my body. I knew changing would happen eventually, but there was no way to be prepared for it.

I finally took a deep solid breath and scooted closer to Cecile. Her blood red eyes look scared and confused, and seeing that tore at my heart. No matter how terrified I was of her, I couldn't let her lay there by herself.

I glanced over at the guys, they stood still, staring from the corner of the room. Typical.

I pulled Cecile up to me in a hug, letting her body relax into mine. I brushed strands of hair off of her damp forehead, as I felt her hot breath against my neck. A slight whimper rang in my ear and she scampered away from me.

Huge eyes filled with fear like a scared child. Her lip quivered and she glanced around the room until she found Drake. Cecile crawled to him and clung to his open arms as she continued to watch me. Why would she choose him over me? How did I scare her more than him? Was I not the right type any more, since I was still human?

Hurt and confusion filled me, but I tried not to let it show. Then she grinned at me, but not a normal grin, this one scared me. Then randomly she slapped both of her hands over her mouth and let out an ear-splitting shriek.

"What's going on?" I yelled over her screams to Cryder.

He came to stand next to me. "She is craving blood."

My eyes shot open. "Oh. Right."

"Right now any blood is tempting." He shrugged.

I started to take a step forward, but Cryder stopped me. "She looks so upset."

"It would be best for you to stay where you are. It won't help to get closer to her, it will only make it worse."

I shivered at the thought that I was making my best friend hurt worse.

Drake lifted Cecile up into his arms like an infant and they whooshed from the room without even a second glance at the two of us.

"How long does that last? She won't always be like that will she?" I asked.

"It could be a few days to a week before she feels completely like herself again. But no she won't always be like that. As long as Drake keeps her satiated she will be fine around you. We will have to keep a close eye on her."

I wrapped my arms around my torso. "You had said that it wouldn't be bad, but she looked terrified and upset."

"Your body is still changing after a few days, but it does go away." He rubbed a hand on my shoulder.

I could feel my stomach somersaulting and I ran to the bathroom. I laid on the bathroom floor letting the cool tile soak into my skin and calm my nerves. While lying there another wave of nausea hit me as I realized I still had to make this same decision. To change into a creature of the night and become a queen.

I brought my knees to my chest trying to relax. I wanted to let everything fall into place, but in the edges of my mind my thoughts were negative. Did Cryder really care for me? Or was this all because he had to? Would I really be accepted by the ancient vampire race at eighteen years old to be their queen?

With Cryder, he made me feel so strong and in control, but completely out of control at the same time. He brought out so many different emotions from me, and no one has ever done that. Something amazing is between us because my heart ached with the thought of him and my body thrummed with excitement by his scent alone, but at the same time my fear of what could or would happen tore at me and halted every decision I thought I could make. Can I jump into it like Cecile, and say yes to Cryder? Could I leave behind the human world? I had plenty of time to make my decision, so I didn't have to worry about jumping into it...right now...

Chapter 10

I didn't sleep that night, I couldn't. Cecile's screams

echoed through the halls. The first one I ignored, but then after

the third one I ran like a kid scared of a thunderstorm to

Cryder's room. I lifted my hand to knock on the door then

stopped. Why was I here? To ask questions, of course, I

answered myself. And so I knocked.

Cryder came to the door in nothing but a pair of boxers, and my chin fell to the ground. All I could see were rippling muscles. Did he have a face? I couldn't remember. I glanced up to see his sparkling blue eyes shine from the moonlight and remembered how beautiful he was from head to toe. A small grin played on his mouth as he stared at me. What was I doing here again?

"Right. Um...hi."

"Are you okay Rena?" Cryder asked in a soft tone.

"Yes, well no. Why is she screaming like that?"

"Her body is still changing. I know it sounds awful, but she shouldn't remember anything by morning. Can you not sleep?"

"Shouldn't? Hell no I can't sleep, Cecile, my best friend is screaming her lungs out right next door to me. Are you sleeping?"

"I was yes."

"Are you use to tormenting screams in your house Cryder?"

"Well no, but I tend to be a deep sleeper. Do you want to go downstairs and I can make you some coffee."

"Right, coffee. You don't happen to have anything mocha flavored do you? I'm sort of missing that right about now."

"Well, it won't be the same, but I'll try to make it as close as possible." He chuckled and grabbed a robe to wrap around himself. Damn. He placed a hand on my lower back while we walked downstairs and a flush filled my body. His touch, oh god, his touch could change the world for me. My heart beat in my ears from his warm hand. The screams had quieted from Cecile, but my heart ached for her. Books didn't lie with this, the change is never something pretty, or sexy. The one thing the media did get right, and it has to be the scariest part of all of this.

* * * * * * * * * *

Coffee with Cryder was great, and we stayed up for a few hours until I couldn't keep my eyes open. Cecile's screams stopped and it was only then that Drake left her side to shower and change. I said hi to him but that was all. There had been too much going on that night, and I still felt hurt that this happened without talking about it or a heads up. Something to say 'Hey, so tomorrow I plan on changing into a vampire.'

I awoke and walked to the bathroom immediately to have the hottest shower known to man and try to erase all the pictures in my head from the previous day. After a while I finally walked out of the bathroom in a cloud of steam, and I could hear Cecile and the guys talking downstairs.

Thrilled as I was to hear Cecile's voice chiming like a bell, I couldn't free the fear clinging to my bones. Would she be different? Would she still want to drink my blood? Is our friendship doomed until I take the plunge and become a vampire myself?

I made my way down to the living room, sucked in a deep breath, and lifted my chin in the air hoping to trick everyone into thinking that I was fine.

I strode in, and all conversation ceased. That awkward moment where you know that everyone was talking about you. I took my seat on the couch and Cryder handed me a mug filled with more coffee. He apparently knew me well. I grabbed the cup from his hands and inhaled the rich aroma. My mouth watered. After I took a sip of the delicious brew, I huskily said, "hi." and then stared at Cryder's hand also holding a mug. "You can drink coffee?"

Cryder shrugged. "I can, not the best tasting anymore. But it's an old habit."

"You used to drink it a lot?"

"It's like a...hmm...how do I say it. It brings a sense of humanity back to me. You enjoy it?"

"Of course. When I was a kid, my grandpa would fill up the creamer cups with his extra sweet coffee and give them to me. It wasn't much, but enough for me to crave it. As I got older it became a ritual. It helps when I'm stressed or freaking out, like now."

That broke all silence and Cryder was by my side in a vampire second. "Are you okay?" he asked.

I only nodded. That question alone made my eyes water. "I'm still me," Cecile responded.

Those words broke the dam. Tears streamed down my face and onto my shirt. "I'm glad," I whispered.

Cecile stood and came over to me slowly. Probably waiting for another ticking time bomb reaction from me. Once she made it and realized I wouldn't run or scream, she sat. "Obviously vampire traits are a part of me now, but I'm not wanting to drink your blood or anything like that." She gave a half smile and I noticed golden flecks in her red tinged eyes. Her fangs weren't showing now as she leaned in to hug me.

I wrapped my arms around her neck. "How are you?" I choked out.

"Fine. Honest. I'm not in pain or crazed for blood, well as long as I'm kept fed. I won't be so desperate for any other. A nice balanced diet of the tomato juice three times a day is sufficient," she laughed. "I'm okay, seriously," she said once she noticed I wasn't laughing.

"Good. I'm glad. I was so sc..." Hiccuped sobs bounced from my chest.

At that time everyone came to hug the last pitiful human in the house...well half-human. Cecile looked sad but she didn't cry, she only held me close. Cryder and even Drake wrapped their arms around me, cooing calming words in my ears until I stopped.

I wiped my face, and stared at Cecile again paying attention to all the differences that had happened over night. She may still sound the same and basically looked the same, but there were still so many changes. "Your hair is longer."

"Yep. And curlier. Apparently another side effect. Positive though, my mountain sized pimple I had growing on my cheek has disappeared," she giggled.

"But that's it?"

"Blemish free. Nicer looking hair. Plus I'm stronger and faster. And I can do this now." She stood up and away from me then snapped her fingers and a red rose appeared in her hand. "Crazy huh?" She beamed.

"You can make things appear?"

"Yep. You can move things, and I can create things. We'll make an awesome team right?" Her smile rose from ear to ear.

"Right," I agreed and tried to smile but my breath caught in my throat. "I think...I need...to be alone..." I forced out.

They all scooted away fro me. Hurt faces on all three of my friends.

"I'm sorry," I whispered. "It's a lot to take in, and very weird being the only human in the house. I just need to breathe my own air for a little while." I stood up and headed toward the foyer, and then made a quick decision that I wanted to go outside and enjoy the hot sun.

I tip-toed through the entry way and headed toward the front door to make my escape. Did I hear footsteps on the other side? I put my hand on the doorknob and the doorbell rang like an alarm system. It yelled out letting everyone know I was trying to escape, or that's what it felt like to me. Who would ring the doorbell to this house? I reached for the knob again to open it, and in a blur Cryder and Drake were in front of me. They blocked me from the door and Cecile stood to my left with a hand on my shoulder.

Cryder opened the door slightly letting a slither of sunlight slip into the house. A pang of fear struck me instantly. Laying in a heap on the front porch was a body.

"There's blood. A lot of it." The aroma didn't smell like Cryder's, it didn't make my mouth water. The only thing this blood did was make me feel sick.

Before I could sneak anymore peaks around Cryder and Drake, Cryder picked me up and carried me in a blur and dropped me onto the couch. "Stay here do not move. It is not safe for you right now." I started to open my mouth to protest, but he put his hand up to stop me. "Please, trust me."

I stopped short and simply nodded. He stood there in front of me looking into my eyes with pure concern, and lifted his hand up to my face then ran from the living room.

I sat on the couch shaking my leg in frustration. I knew he was right. This was not for me to see, but curiosity was seriously killing me. So I stood up and headed to the archway between the foyer and the living room, what would it hurt to check it out? I leaned around the doorway and instantly saw everyone crowding around the body. Blood was everywhere, trailing down the body onto the tarp the guys had apparently brought in to cover the hardwood floor of the foyer.

It took everything in me not to throw my guts up right there in the entryway. I kept reminding myself I was the idiot who decided to come and look. I needed to suck it up and deal now.

I heard a lot of whispering coming from both of the guys, and Cecile sat there staring at the body.

The body, a man, had his chest ripped open. From where I stood I could see his eyes were opened and staring up at the ceiling. His mouth frozen with a grimace, and his fingers curled into fists. His last moments had been spent fighting for his life. I didn't realize I was crying until I tasted salty tears on my lips. Then Drake reached into the torn opened chest, and my gag reflex kicked in. Squishing noises came from inside the body as Drake pulled out a knife connected to a note which was attached to the dead man's heart. That did it, I ran from the room to the bathroom and let my stomach empty itself out.

I sat in there letting the tears free fall from my eyes, and tried to take deep breaths which seemed impossible.

A knock at the door made me jump.

"Rena, are you okay? You weren't supposed to see that you know?" Cecile's sweet voice rang through the door. "Can I come in?"

I sat up enough to open up the door for her, and then plopped back down on the ground.

She came in and sat down next to me, watching me carefully. "Oh man you look awful."

"I don't feel so hot either." I rasped out.

She stood up and grabbed a washcloth hanging on the towel rack and ran it under water before handing it to me and plopping back down next to me.

The warm water felt good on my face. "What did the note say?" I held my breath for what felt like forever until she finally looked into my eyes.

I knew that Cecile couldn't keep secrets from me, and whether it was good for me to know or not know she would let it slip. "The note was...for you Rena. I told Cryder it was good for you to know what was going on."

I tried to swallow down the bile rising in my throat. "What did it say?"

"Here I wrote it down. The paper was drenched in blood."

I scrunched up my nose. "Oh...okay thanks," I said and took the piece of paper from her hands.

Rena, my dear loved one, I have been waiting so patiently to see you again.

I took a deep breath and read the rest of the note, scared to see what else had been written.

I did try to be patient and wait only for you, but then this human tempted me. I ripped through his heart as an example to show your beloved and his people. You belong to me and no other. I will see you again soon, My Queen.

Warmest regards,

Bristol

Cecile wrapped her arms around my shoulders. "It's okay Rena, the guys won't let anything bad happen to you. Plus I'm here to take care of you too."

"I know they will Cecile, that's not what's bothering me. That man, out in the foyer, he died because of me. Because Bristol wants me. I can't be the reason for people dying and just go on. I can't just live life, dammit." My hands shook hard rattling the note.

Cecile nodded at me, then her next words pushed me over the edge. "Relax girly. It'll all be okay. I promise. Drake and Cryder will take care of it all."

My anger started to rear its ugly head inside of me. "Relax? You want me to sit and relax while people are getting killed? People that know nothing about me or even about vampires. He was innocent, Cecile!"

I stood. Cecile held the same scared face that I never wanted to see on her again. Her body pushed up against the wall as much as she could, trying to get away from me.

I closed my eyes, sucked in my breath, and let it all out in one big whoosh. "I'm so sorry Cecile. Everything in our lives has gone from zero to one hundred in a few days, and it's too much for me. I'm sorry." A lump formed in my throat.

She stood up, wrapped her arms around me in a hug, and I laid my head on her shoulder. "It will all get situated, please trust me, and trust the guys. I know it's a lot, but they know more about what's really going on than we do. They won't let anything happen to us." She ran her fingers through my hair trying to help calm my fears.

The comfort of her hands in my hair reminded me of when my mom use to do it when I was little and scared of the monster under my bed. The lump in my throat felt like a baseball now.

I lifted my head off of Cecile's shoulder and looked her in the eyes. "Let the guys know, if you don't I will, that from now on I will be told the truth. I'm just as much a part of this group as anyone else. No matter how I react, I'll still stand back up and face whatever is next head on."

"I'll tell them Rena. You know Cryder won't be happy about all of that."

I nodded and then gave an over-exaggerated shrug. I really didn't care.

Cecile left the bathroom. I knew the guys wouldn't be happy with us, but they would get over it. I splashed some water on my face, staring at my reflection in the mirror. I looked like roadkill ran over twice. My hair fell flat against my head, the simple make-up I had tried to apply earlier was smeared across my face, and my clothes looked like I pulled them from the dumpster. This was definitely not one of my best days. I opened the door.

Cryder stood right outside the bathroom waiting for me. Running right into his tall broad body, I had to bite my lip to stifle a scream. He towered over me as he glanced down at me with true worry in his eyes.

His hand immediately went to my cheek and he gently stroked my face. My breath caught in my throat by his touch, and I could feel myself melting into a puddle right in front of him. His touch could make any fear I had go away in seconds. "How are you doing?"

I put on my best fake smile. "Oh I'm fine. No need to worry." I walked past him toward Cecile, who was talking to Drake.

They both stopped talking once I reached them, and I wanted to scream. I hated feeling like the outsider. "Where's the body?" I asked.

"We got rid of it," Drake answered. He and Cecile were sitting on the couch. Cecile still looked shaken up, but Drake seemed tense. I stepped closer toward them.

"What? You just threw it away like yesterday's garbage?"

"Can't keep him here and have him stinking up the place. Don't worry we'll take care of the big stuff for you."

"Excuse me? What the hell is your problem?" I stood directly in front of him now, my eyes staring right into his.

"You should stay seated in here little girl. This is all too much for a mere half-ling. Queen or not. Maybe once you are all grown up you'll be able to handle all of the grown-up situations, but for now you should sit all of this out."

"Cecile dear, you better get your new boy toy in check. I can't control anything that happens when I get angry, and right now I don't plan on trying." The loud pounding of my heart was all heard by that point.

"Oh please little one, you aren't a match for me, but I would enjoy seeing what you think you could or couldn't do to me," Drake said as he stood up and started to walk away from me.

"Fine." I growled through clenched teeth.

I let the shaking in my hands shimmy its way all through my body. I sprinted to him, and put my hands out towards his chest pushing all of my anger against him. I had expected him to not be affected by my touch. Instead he went flying through the closed front wooden door, through the missed blood splatters, and landed on the porch.

I ran to him and stared into his gray eyes, he glared back. He dusted his pants off with that same expression glued to his face. Drake walked toward the house and bumped into my shoulder as he passed me.

I spun around and yelled before he passed over the threshold. "Drake! Don't you dare walk away you shithead. You come and face me and let's finally get this over with."

"Drake, Rena dammit. You both stop this. You're acting immature." Cecile whined from behind Drake.

"Drake you stop this immediately." Cryder's voice boomed from inside the house.

I came to stand in front of Drake within seconds. We stood face-to-face. "Yeah Drake stop picking on poor little me." I giggled.

He crossed his arms. "Don't touch me again little girl. I'm not going to fight..."

I interrupted him. "You will fight me. I'm tired of your snide remarks and I'm ready to wipe that annoying ass grin off your face. So let's get this over with."

"You two stop now." Cryder started to grab onto Drake.

It was too late. Drake growled and charged toward me like a rabid bull, and all I waited for was the foam to start boiling out of his mouth. He stalked up to me puffing his chest like a blow-fish. My height held no competition toward his, but I wouldn't back down.

He took a deep breath, lifted me with all of the strength, and then threw me. He tossed me like a Frisbee. I flew and stared back into his bright red eyes and could hear Cryder yelling.

I couldn't say how high I had gotten, but he had definitely put a lot more power behind his hit. Drake definitely wanted me gone. I couldn't blame him actually. I wasn't exactly sure why I had gone that crazy besides my vampire emotions were out of control, and Drake just pissed me off.

I wasn't afraid of the flying part until I noticed that I was falling now. I panicked and started screaming. As I came closer to the ground my heart pounded threatening to break free from my chest. I thought I was a going to die of heart attack before I landed.

I somehow bypassed all of the forest trees, but I had nothing to slow my crash. I prayed to whoever would listen, and then blacked out for what felt like seconds.

My body seemed unharmed besides a few scratches. This would be one of the first times I was thankful for the vampire blood running through my veins. I started to stand up, and realized with a startle that I felt an electric jolt run up my body. Bristol was near. I stood still, scared to move. My breathing stopped when I heard his voice slither its way to my ears.

"How nice of you to finally wake up my love." His voice alone sent shivers through my body, and not like the ones Cryder gave me. His words made me feel sick to my stomach.

"Wh...what are you doing here?" I shakily asked.

"I was waiting for you my dear. Actually I was heading to go to you. However, like a miracle you fell into my lap all nice and bloody." Bristol, in one quick motion slid away from the tree he was leaning on, and came to stand in front of me.

"Cryder will be here soon." I could sense him searching for me. He smiled the most terrifying smile I had ever seen, and reached to stroke a long thick finger down the length of my face. I cringed inside but was too scared to back away from him.

"I know. So I won't make this last long." I looked into his empty eyes reminding me of a moonless night. Staring into them created an emptiness to bubble inside of me. "Now that I'm looking at you. Seeing the pink rush to your cheeks and those deep eyes of yours, I think I would rather use you for my benefit. You know? Rather than drink you dry, take your powers, and leave your body for your beloved, I could find a usefulness for you. Well for the time being at least. " He smiled brightly.

I didn't know what to do, or when I had fallen down on my knees in front of him, but I knew I couldn't let him hold my life in his hands.

I stood up. "It's not your choice on whether I live or die. You don't control that, you aren't a god."

His smile faltered, his eyebrows rose and he removed his hand from my face. "Don't be so bold girl. I can change my mind like that," he said with a snap of his fingers.

He quickly had his hand around my throat before I had a chance to turn and run. He pushed me backward, and I landed hard with a thud on the gravel below my feet. He sauntered over to me with a devilish grin. I tried to get up, to run, but I was not fast enough. He slammed my face into the ground and I could hear his heavy breathing at my ear. It mingled with my own ragged breaths.

Bristol flipped me over and he was straddling me with his mouth only inches from my own. A knot formed in the pit of my stomach not knowing if he was contemplating kissing me or killing me. His hand that had been around my throat moved to clasp my mouth shut. He lifted me by the neck and then slammed my head back into the gravel. I tried to fight, but my vision blurred at the edges after that last hit. That was when I felt the next searing pain shoot through me. My body uncontrollably arched upward, as Bristol's knife-sharp fangs penetrated my neck.

Chapter 11

I woke this time in complete darkness. Waking up and being blind to my surroundings is terrifying especially after the night I had. I couldn't catch my breath. I collapsed back into the stiff bed I had been lying on and tried to relax as much as possible. I didn't want to move from that spot, scared of what might be lurking in the corners of the room masked by darkness. Then I realized that I was on a bed, a normal bed with a normal pillow. I hadn't been chained down or tied up. Clips, like movies, popped in my head of what had happened to me before I ended up here. Everything that happened yesterday scrolled through my brain.

Everything came rushing back to me. I yawned, and when I did I had felt a dull pain in my neck, but it stuck out compared to the other aches. I slowly reached to where it hurt and felt two puncture wounds. They weren't bleeding but scabbed over.

Had Bristol chomped into my neck, then decided to bring me back to his place? Was his plan to weaken me, making me wait for him to get hungry again and then drain me? My teeth chattered not from cold but from true fear.

I attempted to stand but failed and stumbled back onto the bed. My eyes adjusted slightly to the darkness and that was when I saw the sliver of light coming from underneath a door. I also noticed then that my clothes had been changed. I was now in boxer shorts and my short sleeved Twilight tee that had Edward's beautiful face on the front. These were my clothes which had been at Cryder's house, I knew I was safe.

Of course I didn't want to think about who out of our little group had actually done the changing. Hopefully Cecile had been a part of the process or else that would add some more stress. Had I put on my pretty lacy panties that morning or was it my laundry day granny undies?

I scooted to the edge of the bed and tried to stand up again, but stopped short when I heard a creaking sound coming from the floor boards outside of the room. The door opened slowly, and a face peered around the tiny opening.

I knew it was him before I could really see his facial features. That was new. To be one hundred percent positive who was standing on the other side of the doorway before even seeing anyone.

My heart raced. Was I excited because it was him?

Cryder noticed I was awake and came strolling into the room. He stood silently by the door.

We stayed silent for a brief moment until he whispered, "I am going to turn on the lights, it may be a bit bright for you. So be prepared."

I nodded, hoping he could see me. Then covered my eyes getting ready to be blinded.

When he flicked the switch, I could feel the brightness of the light on my skin and through my hands. After a minute or two, I finally felt comfortable enough to move my hands from my face, and squinted until I could see. A red tint highlighted the corners of my vision. I assumed it had to do with being in the darkness for so long.

Cryder took a few more slow steps toward me. His eyes searched mine as if he was trying to find some hidden message behind them. I didn't know what he hoped or not hoped to find, but it all vanished when he finally smiled.

His reaction made my heart do cartwheels.

"Oh Rena," he stood in front of me and went to his knees. He then wrapped his arms around my waist snuggling his head into my stomach.

I wrapped my arms around his head gently, embracing the moment. He hugged me like he never wanted to let go, and my breath rushed out of me.

He looked up at me, loosened his grip, but still held on. "I thought...I did not know if I was...I was hoping you would be...I am so happy you are alright." He buried his head even further into my stomach and mumbled, "I'm glad you are awake and healthy. I was hoping that your body could handle what was happening to it." He trembled.

All of his words scrambled through my brain. I tried to put them together so they would make sense. A light bulb exploded somewhere as the realization hit me hard. My hand trembled as it explored my neck to find the two scabby holes.

I then looked down at Cryder and with one hand forced his head out of my stomach and where he could look up at me. He had a few red-stained tears streaming down his face and it made my heart hurt to see him so upset.

I swallowed away the lump forming in my throat and let the words I wanted to say come out of my mouth. "Cryder, am I..." I choked on the word and managed a deep breath to try again. "Have I become a vampire?"

Cryder stood now, towering over me, and grabbed onto my hands. "You have not made the transition, but it will happen soon. I will be here to help you through it." His voice held hope as he spoke to me, but when I looked into his eyes they carried a sadness.

I didn't know what to feel, except fear.

I squeezed his hand and asked, "so what happens to me now?"

I stood there holding onto the last bit of hope I had in Cryder's hand. I stared into the bright blue eyes that held so much love and concern for me, wishing that the only thing I had to worry about was the truth behind those gazes. But the image of Cecile's bright red eyes, sharp fangs, and the conflict she had in her with the desire to drink my blood blurred my vision. Was that how I was going to feel and look? A monster at its truest form?

"Rena," my name came out as a whisper, his breath floating to my face like a warm summer's breeze. He gently caressed my check with his thumb as he held my face in his hands. With his touch a tingle vibrated through my body. "Listen to me alright?" I nodded. "With Bristol's bite he was able to take in your blood. And with him having your blood in his system, he will be able to sense your presence even stronger and always know where you are. The bond will not be like ours, it is not as powerful because he is not your mate, nor will he ever be." The last words escaped Cryder's mouth as a growl.

"No, no, no! He's evil. I don't want him in my head, he's evil!" I kept shaking my head back and forth, back and forth, trying to erase his words from my mind.

Cryder pushed me back at arms length. "I know it's scary. Neither Drake nor I know the extent of Bristol's powers or what all he will do, but we will keep you safe. You must remember that I will not let harm come to you ever again. I should not have let that last tiff between you and Drake even occur, but Cecile and I thought it would be good for you two to let out some aggression. I did not think that Drake would go as far as he did, but his testosterone apparently got the better of him and I am sorry. If it was not for me, you would not be in this situation. Please forgive me." He stared deeply into my eyes, and I found myself being lost in the calming blue sea his eyes brought to me.

All I could do was nod.

He sighed a huge sigh of relief and pulled me to him. "I knew that I had already put you in harm's way once, and I was not going to let this happen again. And if I were to cover some of what he had done to you, then our bond would gain strength and so would you. I could not bear to keep you defenseless. So I did the only thing that I thought would keep you safe, Rena. I bit you."

Those last three words brought me back out of my panicking haze and my body started to shake all over. "So I am changing? You made the change happen? To save me?" My brain worked in overload trying to take in everything he said to me.

Cryder pulled me into him and wrapped his arms around me letting me collapse into his chest.

I wanted the chance to make the decision to change, and now it was going to happen whether I wanted it or not. I didn't have the strength or the want, to lift my head off of Cryder's chest. I asked, "how long do I have, you know until I change?"

"I honestly cannot tell you. For everyone the change is different, even the timing. You saw with Cecile that it happened almost immediately. But for some it can happen overnight or a few days later. As long as you do not fight it. Let the blood take over and let the change happen, and it will be a smooth transition."

I nodded slowly, still leaning into his chest and listening to his heart beat.

After sleeping for who knows how long, I already felt drained and ready for sleep again. I contemplated plopping back into bed and sleeping for the next week or so, but a thought came to me. "How did I get back here?" Cryder's breath increased, but he didn't say anything. So I stepped away from him and looked into those ocean blues which at that moment held nothing but sadness and reluctance. "Cryder? What is it?"

He walked past me to the bed and sat down unable to keep eye contact with me. "I could sense you in the woods, and your fear was stabbing into my heart like a million daggers. I knew I needed to get to you quick, so I ran as fast as I could. But by the time I got there it was too late, Bristol had already sank his fangs into you. Every ounce of my emotions that I carried inside turned to pure blood anger. Bristol and I fought. I fought for you. Bristol laughed the whole time to see me so distraught. It all ended with Bristol's laughter because he knew he had beaten me by being able to over power you, and he ran away as he always does. He did not want to fight me, he only wanted to see the pain in my eyes when I caught sight of what he had done."

My eyes widened with shock. "Why would you go after him? You know how dangerous he is!" It frightened me to think that Cryder had gone against him. After the dead body that had been left on the porch, we knew he was capable of anything. "You shouldn't have done that. His eyes and soul are empty, Cryder. He doesn't care about me except for his own benefit."

He brought his hands to his face. "When I brought you back to the house, I knew I could not let Bristol have such a strong hold on you, so I took everything into my own hands. I'm sorry if you feel that it was the wrong decision, but it was the only way and to give you the strength you will need to survive." With those last words his voice cracked.

I went and sat down on the bed next to him. He kept his face covered. I placed my hand on his knee. "Cryder..."

He lifted his head from his hands, and our faces were only inches apart. My breath sped up and I stared into his blue eyes, then down to his soft looking lips. His faced bent closer to mine.

I gave him my biggest smile and without thinking about it I leaned in and gave him a peck on the lips. A simple kiss, and I could feel my cheeks were a bright cherry red. Before anything could really happen Cecile knocked at the door. Damn. I let out a whoosh of breath I didn't realize I had been holding.

"Oh my bad. Sorry I was just coming in to check on..." Cecile had taken a few steps past the threshold into the bedroom, and glanced over to see Cryder sitting next to me on the bed. Sure enough Cecile's concerned look twisted into a sly grin. "Well I thought you were just waking up but apparently you have been up for a while. Sorry again," she giggled.

"What was that about?" Cryder asked.

"I think she thought other things were happening in here." I laughed loud to hid my embarrassment.

"Other things were happening."

"Yeah, but not what she was thinking."

"Oh, well, not that of course. Not that I don't want...that...I mean we don't have to." He took a deep breath. "You are the only person that makes me this way."

"What way is that?"

"Crazy," he answered.

"Well that's something I guess. Anyway, I guess I need to get up and figure out what happens next."

"I didn't meant that to be rude."

I nodded. "No worries." Yeah right, I thought.

Cryder cleared his throat. "Right. Okay then, see you in a little bit." I nodded again. He left the room to get showered and dressed. What the hell was that, besides the most awkward moment of my life? Immortal vampire, and soon-to-be vampire and we can't even deal with our true feelings. What did he feel for me? I knew what I felt, but I was waiting until he knew-well, until I knew exactly what it was his heart felt for me. Was that pathetic? I didn't care.

I realized I had basically slept a whole day away after the attack from Bristol. The weekend was almost over and I would have to go back to school again in a day, ugh. Would I still be able to go if I had made the change already? Could I still be around people?

After my shower I had to re-apply my powder trying to get rid of the rosy color, of being flustered, on my cheeks but it wasn't helping by that point.

* * * * * * * * *

Downstairs everyone sat at the dining table, but there were no plates set only glasses filled with red liquid. I guessed since this we all knew now what hid in those water bottles, there was no reason to hide it.

"Um...Rena," Drake said.

"Yeah?" No need for politeness to the one that put me in this position.

"I wanted to say sorry."

"Sure Drake. Whatever."

"No really I am. This is all my fault and I never meant for it to get that far." I could see sincerity in his eyes. He hadn't been forced to do this.

"I'm sorry too, man. I pushed buttons that I shouldn't have. We all knew this was going to happen eventually. It just happened a lot sooner that I had hoped for."

"Well if you need anything let me know. I'm at your beck-and-call."

"Oh, really? Sounds great. My clothes need to be washed and I have some shoes that need to be shined." I laughed.

Drake growled. "She's impossible. Can't even take a damn apology for what's it worth."

"I did. A free slave. Thank you. Really." I couldn't stop laughing. Cecile shook her head at us.

"Drake, be seated. We won't have the same things happen again tonight. Rena he was really trying to apologize," Cryder, the voice of reason, said.

"Fine. It's done. Okay? Truce?" I asked.

"Truce." Drake responded with an actual smile on his face.

After dinner we all moved to the family room and collapsed onto the couches with full bellies. Cryder sat beside me with his strong arms wrapped around me, Cecile and Drake were in the love seat across from us sitting in a similar position as us. I looked directly at Cecile and asked, "how much does it hurt?" How much pain would I feel? How long would it take for me to get use to being around humans? These were only a few questions floating around in my head.

She looked at me confused, then recognition hit her followed by sadness. Before she answered me, her eyes went to Drake's. She searched for an okaying nod. He slightly shook his head to her watchful eyes, which I wouldn't have seen if I hadn't been staring straight at him. She opened her mouth to respond, "don't worry sweetie. It will all be fine. Anything you feel before the change, you will forget afterwords. Plus you'll wake up with a superstar glow, it's a fabulous way to wake up." She smiled a ginormous fake smile trying to help me get over panicking, but I knew better.

Cryder's arms tightened around me and I looked into the glowing strength that he sent me through his bright blue eyes. I smiled at him, making me forget for the moment that everyone was dodging my questions. But I couldn't forget. I took a deep breath, smiled at both Drake and Cecile, and pushed away from Cryder. I knew soon I would change, knew I would be in pain, and knew that some time soon I would die and wake up as a vampire. I couldn't just sit there with them. Yes, Cryder's eyes had quenched the strong sense of wanting to punch my fist into the wall or yell at the top of my lungs, but Cecile's no-help answer pushed my buttons some more. Even Cryder had said I didn't need to worry. Didn't need to worry my butt. I was going to change into a vampire, possibly be in pain, and die to wake up into something other than human. And I shouldn't worry?

"I have to go. I guess I'm sleepy. Goodnight everyone." I bowed my head slightly to everyone gave a fake smile and headed upstairs to my room. No one followed. Of course I couldn't go to sleep, all I did was think about changing. How the hell was I suppose to relax now?

So I did the only thing I knew that would calm my nerves and even allow me to feel like sleeping, I went over to the bookshelf that was against the wall at the edge of my bed and picked out some romance book. I think I would be staying away from any vampire books for a while. I laid down to start reading, when there was a soft tap on my door. "Come in."

A few seconds later the door opened and Cryder stood in the doorway. He smiled but it didn't reach his eyes. His golden flecked beautifully glowing blue eyes carried the same sadness I had seen earlier. "Rena," he spoke my name slowly.

I waved him in as I scooted over so we could squish onto the bed together. He came and sat beside me taking my hand in his. "What's going on Cryder? Why do you look so sad?"

"I want you to know that I will be here for you all night. I will not leave your side. I do not want you to go through any of this on your own." He pulled me into him and wrapped his arm around my shoulders. I collapsed into his chest, loving his scent wafting into my nostrils. It brought along a sense of security the second I was near him.

"So what you're saying is that you want to spend the night?" I smiled an angelic smile as my insides burned with the heat of his touch.

He kissed the top of my head and whispered, "what I am saying is that I want you to know that you will never have to go through anything on your own again. I will always be here to help you through."

I looked up into his eyes and smiled. I felt his compassion running through my body. It was peaceful being in his arms. I kissed his soft lips which differed from his tough chiseled body that was surrounding me as we laid in the bed. I didn't hold back as I let my lips engulf his with my overpowering need and want for his touch. We laid there together enjoying our alone time. His arms stayed wrapped around me, my legs were wrapped around him, and I knew if anyone walked in this time they would not be able to tell where I began and he ended.

My eyelids drooped with drowsiness, so I relaxed myself against him and let the need for sleep take over. I drifted off to sleep, and short clips of images popped into my vision. The images weren't scary, but disturbing. I wasn't able to see what was being showed to me.

Then just as abruptly as the images came they were gone. Painful sensations all over my body replaced them. My skin tingled all over, like when your leg falls asleep. My body wouldn't listen to my mind, and I couldn't move or yell out. I was stuck lying in the darkness with a tingling sensation that I couldn't make go away. And again the situation only grew worse. I laid there trying to force myself to move, that only made the tingling turn into a sharper pain. The pain rattled through my organs. My bones felt covered by steel, which kept me from moving. It felt like pure lava had been injected into my veins and steadily made its way from head to toe.

There were cries for help coming from far away, and I wished that I could scream out, but my mouth was filled with something which tasted metallic. A cracking sound filled the room near where I laid, and it sounded like firecrackers were going off. It felt like every bone in my body was being bent in half. Was I dying? Was this the end at eighteen?

The pain shifted and now my whole body felt as if it was being stabbed over and over by needles. I tried to scream but all that came from my throat were gurgling noises. Then my stomach felt like someone had reached in and squeezed it like silly putty. Those invisible hands moved to the next organs it could find to twist and twirled around like a baton. My heart was touched next. Only this time instead of twisting it, the ghostly hands squeezed my beating life until it felt like it would pop, and then it did. My heart exploded, and I wanted to try to fight but I couldn't. I was hidden in darkness being tortured by an invisible force and I couldn't fight back. I was going to die. This was a nightmare come to life. I waited for death to come, and laid with my eyes closed, wondering why death took so long to take me.

Then I remembered...something huge. I wasn't dying, but changing. This was my destiny taking over. My true self being made. I am a vampire.

My foot twitched slightly and I decided to open my eyes. What I saw before me made a loud gasp of awe escape from my lips. I was surrounded by a green grassy field. The field itself was bare, but beautiful. The colors of the grass was the most luscious green. Perfect like a golf course in a retirement town. In this field, flowers were scattered all around creating a rainbow of red roses, yellow daisies and pink calla lilies. Colors of reds, pinks, purples, and yellows surrounded the field. In the very center of this harmonious field sat three distinct rocks.

One large boulder actually sat in the center, with jagged edges surrounding it making the sides of it look as if it swords jutted out. The top however was as smooth looking as marble, appearing as if it had been sanded down to create a relaxing spot in the middle of the beautiful pasture. On the outer most edges, what seemed like they were keeping watch of the area, were large looming trees. Their trunks were so close together and their limbs stuck out in every direction that I couldn't place what limb went to what tree. They acted as security guards for the secluded area. I couldn't see past the tree to even know if there was anything else out there, but at that moment I didn't want to go anywhere else. The weather was nice, and I wanted to revel in the colors surrounding me. I went to the large rock and took a seat on top of it. I wanted to enjoy every little detail before someone came to take me away and onto the next part of death's journey.

Chapter 12

I sat on the rock for what felt like hours, however the weather stayed the same and night never came. Apparently time didn't matter here. I sat a little longer waiting for a sign of some sort to show me where to go, but then an anxious knot filled my stomach. I would have left it alone except that the dull pain turned to a full fledged stomach ache. Someone was watching me.

I climbed off of the boulder and twisted around but didn't see anything or anyone. When I turned back to relax on the rock, eyes stared at me only inches from my own. An ear-splitting scream spilled from my mouth and I tried to run, but I couldn't move. I stood frozen to the spot like a force field held me in place. I quit screaming long enough to realize that the face staring at me belonged to the one monster I'd hoped to never see again. Bristol's normal facial features were distorted now into a full monster mode with fangs and red eyes. I opened my mouth to scream again or do something besides stare at his gruesome face, but his voice stopped me.

"I am only here for you my sweet one. It will always be you, Rena." Bristol's words reached my ears, and my knees went weak. Everything he had done from the first time I felt him to this very second has been focused solely on me.

I crumbled to the ground. Inside of me everything went dark, like a candle being extinguished. I laid there in a broken mess, and Bristol took advantage. He straddled my chest knocking the breath out of me. His hands then captured mine and held them tightly above my head. Why wasn't I fighting back?

He then leaned in letting his fangs scrape against my neck. I felt helpless, and I stopped even trying to fight. I couldn't win and I knew that. I also thought maybe if I gave in, he would leave everyone else alone and his crazy schemes would stop. If I let him kill me everyone else might be safe.

I laid there waiting for Bristol to make his next move, but the same images from before came rushing back to me. Only this time they came slower and clearer. In them I saw a future, my future. The possibility that I did have something to look forward to.

Cryder stood by my side in this vision. Cecile and Drake were with us as well. Smiles on all of our faces, in some place I couldn't recognize. Not only were we happy and together, but we were also surrounded by a large group of unknown people and little kids running around; everyone wearing smiles on their faces. I only knew this was a possible true future because as I smiled my fangs showed, I had become a vampire. The images faded and I felt a little sad to see my happy future disappear.

When I came back Bristol's rancid breath heated the curve of my neck. The candle that had felt like it was blown out lit itself again and the flame burned bigger and brighter. I could feel my strength expanding inside me like a rubber-band. I felt stronger. I wasn't ready to give up and I knew that. I may die one day, but that day was not this one.

I kneed Bristol in the groin. He collapsed to the ground, off of me, and with a girly high pitched squeal. I jumped up quickly, bent over and grabbed him by the shirt collar. I was able to lift this overgrown Goliath off the ground and tossed him like a wad of tissues. I laughed watching him land with a thud in the dirt.

He scampered away from me in fear like a little puppy knowing he was in trouble, all he needed now was a tail to wrap between his legs. I wanted to torture him more, for everything he had done to me and my friends. I wanted to make him feel like defenseless prey.

I stood there watching him try to hide from me. I decided most of all I wanted him gone forever. I wished for the sun to come out from behind the clouds and burn him slowly.

As the thought entered my mind and before it was completely processed, I saw a sliver of sunshine stream out from behind the clouds. The sky that had been threatening rain on this beautiful field, now slid apart allowing more sunlight to caress the grass below. It fell on Bristol, but I was bathed in it as well. But it I enjoyed it, he on the other hand screamed like a baby. I didn't do that, did I?

I put all of my will into ridding the world of this piece of garbage. I shut my eyes tight and asked the huge rocks, that I had been sitting on, to move with speed. I asked them to aim themselves at the evil vampire on the other side of the field.

A scream for help exploded from Bristol, and I opened my eyes. The rocks had left their spot and were now on top of Bristol. He didn't move or yell. he was dead, and I had killed him. How is it possible? My telekinesis had grown so much and the rocks had actually listened. I watched Bristol's body slowly turned to stone. I stood there with morbid fascination as his body fell apart and flew through the wind as dust. I asked the wind to take his body far from this peaceful field. There was no reason he should be allowed to stay.

I felt a crisp cool breeze float past me and watched his remains drift away with the wind. I turned away and laid on my back in the grass letting the sun warm me and loud bursts of laughter exploded from my throat. A humongous weight had been lifted from my shoulders for the first time in a long time, and I would take the time to enjoy it. With the small glimpse of the future, I knew I had a lot to look forward to, and with that peace of mind I closed my eyes and relaxed with a smile on my face.

* * * * * * * * * *

I awoke to darkness, as always, but with a knowing that I was safe. I unwrapped the blankets tightly tucked around me, and felt a nuzzle against my neck. Turning, I realized that Cryder's features popped out even in the dark as he watched me stretch. His eyes glowed in the darkness, the gold flecks stood out making his eyes shine like stars.

I could feel the difference as the new blood pumped through my veins. My heart raced but in beat with Cryder's now, which I could hear pumping as he laid next to me. Vivid details of the room stood out to me. Cracks and holes in the walls were noticeable now. I could read every title of every book sitting on the shelf.

"Your timing is perfect my love." His words softly caressed my ear and sent chills down my body.

I smiled rolling onto my side to face him. "Oh yeah? Why is that?"

He lightly stroked his fingers down my neck down to my collar bone and back up. "Because the sun has set and the moon has risen, which means it is time for vampires to awaken."

In a blur I sat up in bed, feeling stupid for not immediately understanding. Why the golden specks in Cryder's eyes glowed so brightly with a burning intensity, and his breath alone when it touched my skin created noticeable goosebumps. It all was more intense because I had become a vampire. The change had taken place while dreaming, and I briefly remembered the pain. I knew I had felt it, but not how bad it had gotten. The same strength I had felt in the field followed me now. So it was a dream? "Is it normal to dream while you are changing?" I asked. "Oh and is everything always this intense too?" I wondered, shivering as his lips caressed my earlobe.

He laughed angelic music to my ears. "Yes your senses are heightened even more after the change. You will only learn to control them all after time, but the strong feeling- that will not go away." He laughed again as he left a trail of kisses down my neck.

My whole body trembled this time adding a fire burning sensation in my lower abdomen. I pushed away from him and got out of bed before turning to him to speak, "well, aren't we getting cozy?" I giggled. "You are going to have to stay away from me for a little while until I learn to control my...um...well urges."

Cryder's eyes watched me, passionately, making my knees wobble but I forced myself to concentrate on my first question. "So do you normally dream during the change? Because I remember that part vividly."

He nodded still staring at me, trailing my body from head to toe with his eyes.

"Well, is the dream normally about the vamp that wants you dead?"

Cryder sat straight up in bed and before I knew it he was at my side with his hands holding my shoulders. "What? You dreamed about Bristol?" He asked with a furrowed brow. I nodded. "Close your eyes tight."

I did as he said. He flipped the light switch and I waited a little while before opening them. The light stung for a few seconds but then my eyes adjusted again.

"Tell me your..." His words were cut short, he had stopped talking and only stood there staring at me. A broad smile formed on his lips.

"What is it? Why are you looking at me like that? Do I have something on my face? Oh bed head huh? Is it bad?" He laughed a throaty laugh.

"I am looking at you because you are beautiful beyond words. Your eyes are glowing now, a hazel color with the same gold speckled through them. There's a mirror in the top drawer of the night stand."

I walked over to the night stand, noticing that my hand shook as I lifted the mirror to see my face, and the reflection looking back at me wasn't familiar. She was a stranger. Her skin was blemish free, her eyes shimmered as a bright hazel with a hint of red at the edges. The color had changed in her hair as well. Still dark brown but now golden highlights brightened the color surrounding her face. The length of her hair was longer than mine too. It was thicker and hanging down to my hips with a wave in it. Her teeth straighter and little pockets in her gums showed evidence of fangs sitting and waiting to be used.

"What do you think?" Cryder still watched me. I'm sure he waited for me to go crazy and get excited, but I couldn't.

Too much had changed in me to jump for joy with not have pimples anymore. I took a deep breath and tried to calm myself. "Well it's me I guess. But isn't me at the same time. I don't know, this is a lot to take in right now." I sat back down on the bed, feeling a wave of nausea roll through my stomach.

"It is still you Rena." He came and sat next to me putting his hands on mine. "You are still in there. I promise." I nodded and forced a smile on my face. Too much at once was all I kept thinking. "So tell me about your dream." His eyes took on an intense look again as he waited for me to give him the details.

Where do I start? "Well I had landed in this gorgeous field filled with different types of flowers and different colors all over. I was alone for a while, enjoying the beautiful sight, and then all of a sudden Bristol was there." I continued and told him of being filled with an insane strength, something that told me to get up and fight. I told him about the watching Bristol's body harden into stone and then collapse to dust and all the while he sat there with a straight face and listened to every word that came out of my mouth. "So I guess it's not normal to dream about killing someone?"

"So you killed him? And moved the rocks with your mind, or actually you called them boulders right?" I nodded. "Hmm... Okay then that is different, but if that is what you saw."

"It was just a dream Cryder." He sat there only staring at me. "Why are you looking at me like that?"

He shook his head as if to clear his thoughts and then glanced down at our hands which were still intertwined and sitting in my lap. "This dream you had concerns me for many reasons, but the main one is that our dreams that we see as we go through the change are normally given to us to show the future. Which means in your future you are destined to fight Bristol, and apparently on your own." He shuttered that time and closed his eyes taking a deep breath. "That last part is what I do not like and will try to avoid at all costs. I do not wish for you to fight someone so dangerous ever."

"Well I guess the only good thing with all of this is that I kicked Bristol's ass, and it felt good. Plus I made him squeal like a little girl!"

Cryder's eyes lit up. "To be able to maneuver those large rocks with just your mind is a very strong power."

"Yeah I think I may have controlled the weather. But I'm not completely sure."

"To control weather is a lot of power in one vampire. You can control whether all vampires get to walk free without sun, or if death will come to them. Let's not say anything until we know for sure. Okay?"

"Yeah I got it. Its not exactly something I want to brag about"

"Good then, how about you and I get cleaned up because I think that Drake and Cecile have put together some decorations to welcome you as a full fledged vampire."

I laughed and shook my head all at the same time. "Great a 'congratulations on becoming part of the undead' party. How fun," I said sarcastically.

Cryder smiled, kissed my forehead, and then left the room. I sat on the bed a little longer, trying to put my thoughts in some form of order.

A possible battle to the death between Bristol and me, plus a new power that could possibly be considered dangerous and put me as an enemy towards other vampires. And now I was a vampire. Throughout the day I had changed and I still didn't know how to feel about it. I thought that I would scream or go mad or cry, but I didn't do any of that.

I finally forced myself to head to the bathroom and take a shower, which felt amazing! I never knew a shower could feel so good, but with my senses being heightened my nerve endings were on over-drive. The water that trickled down my skin felt like a massage. I loved it.

* * * * * * * * *

I made my way downstairs and stopped to stare at all of the decorations that Cecile had put up. Hundreds of helium filled balloons floated against the ceiling, bright neon colored streamers hung down covering the doorways, and signs with different sayings were tied off between the archways. Signs that read: 'Congratulations' and 'Welcome Home' and the other one I saw which I guessed made some sense to this situation said 'Happy Birthday'.

I laughed but it made me feel giddy and ready to spend time with my friends, and boyfriend. Is that what he is now? What do you call a vampire you have strong feelings for, and you think he has the same feelings for you?

I made it all the way down the stairs about to walk into the living room when I caught sight of the reflection of the stranger, supposedly me now. I gawked at her as she gaped back at me. My hair or her hair, whichever, had just recently been drenched by water in the shower and was already dry from root to tip. It waved perfectly at my hips. I didn't take the time to put any make-up on, and yet it looked like I had spent time on fixing myself up. My cheeks had a rosy tint to them, my eyes outlined by black as well as a deep brown color tattooed my eyelid. My lips puckered with a strawberry red.

The color made me think of blood, and with the thought of blood my stomach rumbled. I ignored it, stuck my tongue out at the rude copycat in the mirror who mimicked my exact motions, and walked away.

I walked to the living room, which apparently was suppose to be holding a surprise party. The one where everyone yells 'Surprise!'. It ended up only being Cecile yelling while the guys stood and gawked at me.

"Whoa." Was Drake's response, followed by a smack from Cecile on his arm, which was followed by...

"I know," from Cryder and a smirk on his face.

I laughed but briskly walked to the couch and away from all the attention.

"Looking hot girly! I may actually be feeling a smidgin of jealousy, not much though." Cecile laughed.

I rolled my eyes at her.

Cryder walked over to me, wrapped me in his arms, and dipped me backwards to give me a huge sloppy kiss. I laughed but blushed. The moment was nice. Having the people closest to me there and everyone wore smiles. No drama between us. This had to be the calm before the wild shit storm that would soon bombard my close to perfect world.

It was time to buckle up, because it's going to get bumpy.

Chapter 13

With being transformed into a full-fledged vampire I thought I would be more terrified. I figured fear would've consumed me. Instead I spent the night learning how to fight, how to be quick on my feet, and how to use my powers like a vampire. Everything clicked. I could fight like a ninja once I got use to my new body. My powers still needed work, but I could use them continuously now. The coolest part was when I was able to get my water bottle to come to me from the kitchen to the living room. Talk about lazy-coolness.

With all of that going on I thought that I would be dismissed from human lifestyles, but Cryder still forced me to get up early. He made me get in the car with Cecile and demanded that we go to our classes. Well, he was nice about it, but I still felt pushed into doing something I didn't want to do. There were more important things in life at that moment, in our lives at least. They could possibly be of apocalyptic proportions and we needed to take care of them. However, instead of listening to me, Cryder packed my lunch special with some elixir to keep me fed so I wouldn't attack anyone, and then he wished me a good day.

"Okay, so don't forget to drink the stuff, and keep it handy all day. Try to ration it out to last till the end of classes. Be nice to everyone, but act your old self. Don't try to over do yourself. Meet me at lunch in our usual spot. If anyone asks about where we've been since we missed last Thursday and Friday, just say I had the flu and you were there to help. Got it?"

"Yes mom," I sarcastically answered.

"I'm just trying to help. I didn't have to come to school when I changed. So I have major respect for you right now. It's going to be rough, but you're a tough chick. We have first period together but after that you're on your own. Find me if you need anything."

I nodded. We made our way to class and I tried to embrace the normal me. Lately I had become nothing but serious, so I had to find the not so serious me again.

The first bell rang and I stood frozen. A fear ran through me. I panicked and this time it didn't have to do with any impending doom. This fear only had to do with the change and the delicious aroma of young innocent blood wafting around me. I could sniff out the purest and cleanest blood, the ones that would fill me and give me the energy that I needed. There were also the ones that were filled with emotions and wonderful humanity that if I drank from them I myself would be grounded to Earth by their humanity. What the hell was I talking about? The longer I stood there letting my nose bring in the the most amazing scents, the stronger my desire was getting and the dryer my throat felt. I had been squeezing the lunch pack, which held the elixir, to my chest. I turned around and walked away.

"Rena? Rena, where the heck are you going?" Cecile asked as she followed me. "Are you okay?"

"Stupid," I muttered.

"What?"

"Nothing. I need to get away. The blood, their blood...I can smell it. Taste it. I need the elixir, now."

"Okay let's head back to the car. You'll be fine. It happens. I mean you saw me all..." She mimed fangs and started to laugh but stopped as soon as she looked straight into my eyes. "Oh wow. Don't...don't worry Rena, we'll get you home soon. "

I gave her a confused look and she handed me a mirror. The stranger looking back at me had pale skin. Her rosy pink cheeks had vanished. In fact they were sunken in, and her eyes were nothing but dark circles. The beautiful golden specks and hazel color that I tried to accept were now a vibrant blood red. I looked like a vampire. A true creature of the night. Tears stung my eyes. That reflection belonged to me, and at that second I hated it and hated what I had become. I through the mirror to the ground. Sobs escaped my throat, which at that moment was dry and aching. I felt like I had been walking through a desert for days without any water. Except water wouldn't quench my thirst now.

"Oh, don't panic Rena. That will only make it worse."

I realized then that Cecile had been half-walking and half-dragging me through the school grounds. She made sure to keep me from being seen by anyone. I collapsed into the passenger seat of her car and let it lay back as far as it would go. "Hang on just a little longer okay? I'll get you home as fast as I can."

I could feel the drive as I was thrown against the door and then back against Cecile. She drove recklessly for me, trying to get us home. I nodded. That was all I could do. My stomach started burning. The pain hit so hard that I curled onto my side. I heard a scream that sounded like it was coming from outside the car.

I didn't realize that was me screaming until Cecile patted my arm whispering. "Sssshhh...you will be okay I promise. We are here. I know it hurts. But you will be taken care of."

"I'm...a...monster." I said through gasping sobs. Cecile shook her head.

"No you're not it's only a phase, you will be back to being gorgeous you again, once you are fed." She got out of the car and I felt like I was going to pass out. I could feel myself fading as her arms slipped around me.

Someone else helped to pick me up out of the car, thick and masculine arms wrapped around me. My energy was completely drained from the blood lust, and my eyes fell closed.   * * * * * * * * * *

I walked into this knowing that I was asleep, but that didn't stop the fear from swarming my body or the sweat bead across my brow. Something about this dream filled me with dread and a need to run away. It wasn't necessarily the surroundings, because it was a crisp fall day and I sat on the front porch of some old dilapidated cabin. The woods surrounded the abandoned building.

Seeing the sun in this dream created a little bit of fear in me. Newborn vampires can't withstand the sun for too long, but it didn't seem to affect me here. I had a feeling someone watched me from the woods. I could feel eyes following my every move.

I heard *his* voice.

"Why hello there sweet one. I have been waiting for an opportune time to speak with you one on one. I have missed you."

Bile rose in my throat. Bristol missed me? I hated the thought of him period, and to know that he thought about me at all disgusted me.

"What the hell are you doing here? This is my dream. Leave me the hell alone."

"Is it your dream? Are you completely sure of that?" He stood on the porch now.

I stood now, at the line that crossed into the woods.

Was I sure that this was my dream? This place didn't looked familiar, but then again neither did the field. But I didn't feel powerful here or at peace like I did in my last dream.

I didn't want to know why or how Bristol brought me here.

"I am pleased that you know I'm not lying to you. Your blood is in my system. As long as it's there I can find you wherever and whenever I want. That includes while you're sleeping. Even though I can feel Cryder's strength flowing in you, which means our bond isn't as strong as I would hope for." He shrugged. "As long as I have any hold on you my plan will work."

"What plan?" My legs trembled.

He smiled. "You have decisions you will have to make as the time goes on. Deciding what side you really want to be on, and whom you want to be with. There are consequences for each decision, and I want to show you exactly what you will face with each." He had taken a few steps off of the porch and closer to me.

I started to back up. "Of course there are consequences for my decisions. Every action has a reaction. I've learned my lesson from early on. I couldn't possibly think of anything that you can show me that will push me to cast a vote to be on your side."

He scoffed at my words and shook his head. "I want you to see the truth so you can know exactly what you will have to face in the future."

"Fine, I'm assuming that even if I don't want to go through with this you're going to make me. So let's get this crap started."

"There is no need for snide remarks. I am doing you a favor by letting you see this. I didn't have to do this, but you should see. You might end up liking my side better."

I couldn't hold back my laughter. How could I ever go against Cryder and choose to be with Bristol? That was insanity at its highest peak.

Bristol put his hand out for me to hold. I took the few steps that brought me closer to him, and had to fight the urge to run from his empty gaze. His midnight colored eyes had me on the verge of going mad. I could see the end of the world in his soulless black holes, and it was an awful view.

"Why do I..."

He cut me off. "It's a necessity for you to see the truth." He pulled me to him, wrapped his arms around me, and I struggled inside to not scream. "This, my dear, is your life if you were to choose me. If you were decide that what you really wanted was to fight the big fight on my side. Let humans fall and vampires rise." He gestured for me to walk through the door.

I gulped in a large ball of air and walked past the threshold.

Inside the cabin, all of the rotted walls had evaporated, and now the building had become a castle. Spiral staircases intertwining through each other going up at least three stories, beautiful landscape paintings hanging on the walls, and ginormous gold-lined sparkling crystal chandeliers hung from the ceiling.

I stood alone in a large foyer. I had planned on standing there until I woke up, but then I heard laughter coming from a room nearby. It wouldn't have grabbed my attention, except that it was me laughing.

I took a step toward the sound.

A different me sat on a couch wearing some skin-tight gaudy purple sparkling dress. My hair was curled to perfection. I was laughing and staring lovingly at a man who sat on the couch next. The golden speckles I had grown accustomed to were gone, in their place were bright blood red eyes.

I couldn't see the man's face, because it was turned away from me. He had wide broad shoulders expanded out past the couch's arm, and long messy dark hair. His words whispered from his lips and I realized I had been relaxing with Bristol.

I walked around to actually look at the other me. My legs drooped lazily over his lap, and his hands snaked their way up and down my thighs. A smile plastered on both of our mouths nearly threw me back. I couldn't imagine anything sicker than having the beast I despised touching me the way he was.

The other me leaned to the opposite side from Bristol and mashed a button on the table next to the couch. In an instant, Cryder came bursting through the door. My heart beat faster than normal by seeing him and I rushed over to him. But my body floated straight through him like a ghost.

His clothes were torn and holes covered his pants. Normally his hair spiked perfectly atop his head now laid flat and greasy. His eyes appeared so lost and forlorn. It made me hurt to see him that way even in a dream.

Cryder ran up to the other me and knelt down on one knee. "How may I assist you my mistress?" Mistress?

"We require sustenance servant." As I stood there watching in utter disbelief, Cryder nodded, stood, and pushed the sleeve up on his shirt to offer the vein in his arm for other me to drink.

I stifled a scream as the other me sank her fangs into the thick vein on his wrist. Cryder let his head roll back and a moan of pleasure released itself from his throat. Bristol drank from the other me and moans of excitement rang in my ears from the three feeding vampires.

The scene skipped ahead to a new scene like someone had pushed a button on a DVD remote. This time, still in the palace, two little boy vampires ran around chasing each other. They had dark curly brown hair, with a stocky build. Cryder ushered them from one room to the living room.

"Where's mommy?" one little boy asked Cryder.

"She's in there waiting for you."

I stood in the foyer still staring at the children. Their faces lit up as they found their mother. I ran up behind them, and watched as they fell into...my arms. The same other me held them. The two children had sly smiles on their faces, and as I tore away from those eerie smiles I stared into their eyes. They were as soulless and empty as Bristol's.

Those evil eyes glared at me and I ran from the room.

I ran to the foyer where I had originally started this rancid dream and huddled into a corner. Not wanting to see these images any longer, I shut my eyes as tight as they could go. A strong wave of nausea weaved its way into my stomach. I took slow normal breaths and opened my eyes to find that I now stood in the cabin with Bristol. "Wh...what...was that?" I placed a hand along the wall behind me to keep from collapsing.

"That is how life will be if you choose to be with me. Does it not seem delightful? You could have everything you ever wanted, with a simple press of a button or snap of your fingers."

"That's nowhere near what I would define as delightful you deranged lunatic. You're delusional and insane if you think I would ever choose that." Anger's dark tendrils climbed its way up my body.

"Fine, you think there could be something better. Let me show you your other choice of life, and you will see why I am the best one for you."

The air around me began to shimmer causing the cabin to disappear. This time I was in darkness.

Whispers rose from behind me and I whirled around. Allowing a few seconds for my vampire eyesight to kick in, I was in an alley way. A figure covered in dark clothing stood near me. She was a female from with a small frame of her figure. She hunched over and stared at some item on the ground. Before I could make it over to where she crouched she buried her face into the object. A ripping sound filled the silence in the alley way. Slurping followed and even though I knew I didn't want to see, my curiosity beat out any common sense running through me.

I squatted in front of her as she lifted her face. A gasp flew from my lips as I saw the blond curly locks that belonged to my best friend. Her greenish-golden eyes showed no other color now except for a glowing blood red. Cecile had red drool dribbling past her chin as she stared at the rat in her hands. Blood stained her pale skin. Sobs racked my body as I sat there unable to do anything but watch.

A shuffle of feet came up behind her. Drake came to a stop directly behind Cecile. "I am back Cecile. I am here for you my love."

A hiss came from Cecile at Drake's words. "Where have you been? You said you would come back a month ago. I'm so hungry."

"Ssh my love, I know, and I am sorry. The war is still going and I have been on the front line with the others."

"Are Rena and Cryder still alive?"

"Yes they have survived so far, but the rogues are getting stronger and we are losing people left and right."

"As long as Rena is okay. That's all I'm worried about. I know she will take care of all of this, and then we can go back to what we were."

A tear trickled down my face at the thought of my poor friend being so helpless. I wasn't sure what had brought her to this point, but this was awful to watch.

"She is. Cryder stands with her and their children are helping with the injured. They are doing what they can to bring us back to how we were before Bristol started this war against the humans. We even have human soldiers standing with us, however they aren't much help against rogue vampires." Drake stooped down and lifted Cecile from under her armpits like an infant child, and then brought his neck to her mouth. She hesitated for only a second before she sank her fangs deep into his flesh. Then in a haze the image switched to what I assumed to be the battle field.

Cryder and I stood front and center throwing out orders to the others. They all fought with such effortless movement. Still many fell to their deaths in the same graceful elegance that they fought with. The smell of blood filled the air.

Wounds covered our own bodies, but the determination in our eyes was so strong. A fatal blow had been given to Cryder, and then to me. We fell to the ground as a pool of blood surrounded us and the gold in our crowns shimmered from the moonlight as they toppled off of our heads.

Bristol bent down on one knee at our bodies and filled a goblet with our blood. Once the glass over flowed with our life's source, he allowed his creatures to burst through like a herd of buffalo and swarm our bodies.

I couldn't stand to watch any more, the rancid bile sitting in my throat since the beginning of these visions pushed its way out. I hunched over, retching away from the slurping and sucking noises. I cried out, tears streaking down my face in sheets.

The sounds behind me began to fade, but I still continued to cry out. In between my quick intake of breaths, I heard laughter. The cold humorless sound that could only belong to one evil creature.

Bristol's laughter overpowered my sobs, and his words rang out in surround sound. "Now you tell me which is better in the end. What will be your final choice?"

Chapter 14

My screaming startled me awake. I shot out of bed. The tears in the dream had followed me to the real world. My face and the collar of my t-shirt were drenched with my salty tears. Cryder had slept next to me and flew out of bed the second he heard my screams. He stood by my side, not touching me, but I could feel him watching over me. Having him there calmed me. The visions shook me up inside.

I could still hear Bristol's words. *"What will be your final choice?"*

Both scenarios were awful, and there was no good choice from what he offered. In both, Cryder was doomed as a servant or death. Could I push him into a future that I know will be the death for us? Could I spend my life in the clutches of evil as Cryder spends his days as my servant? Would it not be better to fight side by side for what we believe in till death, rather than live in a life that would be a true living hell?

"Are you alright?" Cryder's voice made me break away from my inner struggle.

"It was a nightmare. Bristol was in it." I didn't want to tell Cryder every detail.

It was just a dream right?

Cryder wrapped his arms around me and pulled me into his warm body. My breathing slowed to a natural pace.

I slid my arms around his thin waist and let my body melt in with his.

"I thought infusing my blood with yours would cancel his hold on you. I apparently was wrong in my thinking," he said.

"How can I break him loose and make him go away?"

"The only way I know of breaking that bond is by killing the one you are bonded with. Normally I would say that killing to break a bond isn't the way to go, but in Bristol's case I don't see a problem with it."

I pulled away from his arms. Making my way to the bedroom door, I turned back to him and said clearly,

"This fight is against Bristol and me. And if death is what it will take, then death it will be."

* * * * * * * * * *

We tried our hands in actual fighting between the four of us. The guys tried to help us relax and learn our true speed. Plus we got a chance to dabble a little in our special powers.

"Breathe, love. Relax. Do not force it. Let it come naturally. That is what you did before. Your natural raw emotion is what caused your power to emerge." Cryder sat on the couch watching me try to move items around the room with my mind.

I only nodded. In my mind I attempted to picture something or someone to bring out the most emotion from me. Bristol's empty maddening eyes popped first into my vision. Followed by the rest of his disgruntled face. His lips pulled up into the grimace he normally held letting his fangs show. With this image I could feel boiling anger stir inside me.

I opened my eyes and heard a gasp come from somewhere in the room. My eyes didn't focus at first and when they did they stuck to an object in the room. My eyes laid on a small red lamp placed on the coffee table. In my mind I told the lamp to rise. The lamp shook and slowly rose from the table top. I then willed it to float across the room. It floated to across the room, and I asked it to land softly on the fireplace mantle and it did just that with a soft thud.

I collapsed to the ground, gasping for breath, feeling a large amount of energy drain out of me. Cryder stooped to lift me from under the armpits, and brought me down onto the couch. I let the leather form around my body as I relaxed into it.

"You did it," Cryder whispered to me.

I gave a small smile and attempted to sit up.

"You're a queen in training and its obvious that there's some serious power inside of you. When you got angry your eyes went all scary and red." Cecile stood in the archway of the living room.

My head jerked up to look at her. "What? Really?" I turned to look at Cryder. Concern filled my voice. "Is that true? That's bad isn't it? I mean I don't feel very powerful right now."

He shook his head. "No my love, it is that power inside of you wanting to come out. Once you learn to harness it, it will not be so overwhelming." He caressed my arms slowly. "Let me get you something to drink. Rest."

I sunk back into the comfort of the couch. Drake followed Cryder to the kitchen and Cecile came to sit next to me. We sat in silence for a few minutes.

I caught my breath and Cecile watched me with worry on her brow. "What is it Cecile? Why do you keep watching me like that?"

She hesitated for a brief second, staring at her pink painted fingernails. "I'm just concerned that's all. Like Cryder said, there is a lot of power in you but it's almost as if you are stopping it from coming out. Those eyes you had for like a split second showed that you are strong, but if you don't let it happen I'm scared to see what might happen to you."

I felt my face squish up in confusion as I stared at her. "What do you mean? Happen to me?"

"Well you know like when someone has so much something in them and they don't let it out they can maybe like...explode. What if all that power in you doesn't get harnessed?"

"You think I might explode?" Now I was beyond confused.

"No not quite, well maybe...I don't know. Maybe if you don't control it, your eyes will stay permanently red, and the power will control you so you won't be you anymore. You know?"

"Oh my goddess if you keep talking like this I'm going to freak out even more than I already am."

She fiddled with her hands some more. "I'm just scared that you aren't going to be able to let go and control the power yourself, that it'll start to control you. That you'll become the scary queen type. That you'll end up fighting against us and not with us."

Her words slammed into me. An image from the visions popped up, and I saw myself again on the couch with Bristol laughing and staring lovingly at him with my beady red evil looking eyes. Had Cecile seen something too?

"Um...yeah maybe you're right...maybe I just need to take a breather and try again later," I agreed.

She nodded seeming more relaxed by my answer.

"I think I'm going to step sit on the porch and get some fresh air. I won't go far. It might be just what I need to calm down and concentrate." I smiled at her.

"That sounds good, you've been stuck in here ever since the whole school fiasco." She patted my leg and smiled at me encouragingly.

I went to the front door, and slowly stepped outside. The air was cool. The wind blew, playing with my hair, blowing it every which way. Although it may have been a cold night my skin couldn't feel the chill. Apparently vampire skin couldn't feel the differences in the weather because I knew winter would come soon but it still felt like crisp fall air to me. I found it enjoyable not having to worry about a jacket or bulky sweaters.

I decided to go to my car and grab some CD's from the car. That always helped to relax me. I took my sweet time, enjoying being alone. Opening the door I bent over to dig through my music selection and straightened up quickly when I heard a crunching noise behind me. I couldn't ignore the fact that my stomach did cartwheels.

Fear wouldn't let me turn around and face him. He was getting closer and with the breeze that had been blowing came a strong scent of vampire. Not just any vampire, but Bristol's stench blew toward me.

I wanted to face him and not give into my fear but I was shoved up against the car. My arms were pulled and forced painfully behind my back. A blindfold covered my eyes, and he wrapped a thick rope around my wrists. I started to scream, but then felt hot breath steaming against my neck.

His slimy voice slithered up to my ear. "I knew I would get you alone at some point, my dear queen." He spat out the last word in hatred.

Fear spiraled its way from my stomach and up to my throat. I tried to struggle against his body but he pulled my arms up causing a fierce pain to shoot through my shoulders. I wanted to scream, but nothing would come out. Cotton filled my mouth.

"It would be wise if you didn't scream or struggle against me. I won't hesitate to kill you on the spot and then do the same to your friends inside." He gestured toward the house. "However before your death comes, I have a proposition to run by you. Please move quickly and quietly and nothing bad will happen for now." He laughed.

A whimper escaped from my mouth, but I gave a small nod and let him drag me away. Bristol had finally found me, and came to take his revenge.

He yanked my body in the direction he wanted me to move. His scent blasted me in the face. He smelled exactly how a living corpse would, a mixture of death and decay. My feet barely skimmed the ground while he drug me along. I was beyond terrified, but I had to try my best to stay calm. His anger had a short fuse, and he was bound to go off at any time. I kept my mouth closed, and let him take me.

I didn't want to let Cryder know anything about what was going on, because I didn't want him to come rushing in and get killed. Bristol was the epitome of evil, and wouldn't be afraid to strike at anyone that tried to get in the way of his plan.

When I could get out of the path of his scent, I smelled

pine trees surrounding us. He took me further into the woods.

Eventually we came to a dead stop, and his hold on me

dropped. My excitement was short lived as he wrapped one

arm around my shoulders and the other underneath my legs.

Hoisting me up in his arms, he walked up a few stairs and

opened what sounded like an old wooden door.

"Let's get this shit outta the way. I'm tired of all the

games. It's boring." I knew I was being gutsy, but I wanted to

know why he hadn't killed me yet.

"We will get to that point soon my dear. We have many

things to discuss."

I cringed inside feeling sick with the endearing terms,

and with how calm he was acting now. The nightmare

continued playing in my mind. I knew he wouldn't kill me now,

if he had any hope that in the end I would choose him. We

walked into a room which smelled strongly of mildew and rot.

"Oh my god what is that smell?" "Shut up." His grasp on

me tightened.

"Keep your mouth shut until I am ready to talk to you."

The stench filled my nose, Bristol had smelled the same. He threw me onto something that was soft to the touch. I leaned back and the item leaned back with me; a rocking chair of some kind. I was grateful to be out of his arms, and in a chair instead of some weird jail cell, which I had envisioned in my head.

The chair reclined back, and my legs lifted straight up. Bristol's hands slid down my legs and his rough touch made me squirm. I didn't want his hands or any part of him touching my bare skin. His fingers made their way to my ankles and his grasp tightened holding them together while he tied them together. He also tied my legs down to the chair.

"I don't know what powers you've been given after your change, but I'm not taking any chances." Bristol said as he finished making the last knot around my legs.

"I understand why you're doing this, and I'm sorry for everything you had to go through. I really am."

Plan: keep your enemies closer.

"That's very touching that you're trying to be nice to the beast holding you hostage, but you will never understand the honest reason why I'm doing all of this or what's truly going on in my mind. So shut it now, or I will gag that delicious looking mouth of yours."

Plan: failed. "Is there anyway I could get some water or something to drink? My throat is so damn dry."

A noise came from Bristol that sounded more like a hiss, but it was him laughing. "Of course sweet one, I have exactly what you need."

His footsteps thudded along the wooden floor. A strong and delicious scent then caught my focus, it had my mouth watering as it dribbled into a glass. The smell intrigued me. It was slightly spicy but very fruity at the same time. I knew the smell but the fragrance wafted to my nostrils and nearly knocked me back. My craving for this drink was unbearable, and although I knew exactly what I was about to devour I couldn't stop my need for it. My stomach growled for it.

He brought the drink closer, and I took a deep breath. Bristol placed a straw in my mouth and I gulped down every drop. Then the straw slurped back letting me know that the cup was empty.

"Whose bl...blood did I just drink?" I could feel my heart threatening to bust past my rib cage. I was going to be sick. How could I have been so stupid?

"Oh that was my blood. Made specially for you."

"How could that taste like that to me?"

"You mean why did it taste good?" I nodded hesitantly. "Because you have recently changed. Blood, any blood is good to you right now. It makes me feel good that you enjoyed it." He chuckled.

My stomach somersaulted at his words. With his blood now in my system, he would have a stronger hold on me. He could already read my thoughts and invade my dreams, but now he could be in control of me. Make me long for him, crave his blood, and cause me to feel his emotions.

The ritual isn't the same when you do it with someone you aren't destined to be with, or that's what Cryder had explained. I had become his substitute mate, and he was mine. If I continued to drink his blood, I would eventually go mad like him.

Cryder was a bond-mate so his power over me was stronger than Bristol's ever could be, but I was still obligated to both in different ways. I hated this and it was all my stupid fault. I knew what had to be done. I had majorly screwed up and felt like vomiting every last drop of Bristol's blood. It wouldn't help because the energy from his life's source was already merging with my blood. Tears stung my eyes from the fear of what this could mean. I blinked hard to keep the water works from starting up. I needed to come up with something fast, because I was not going to sit here and let myself fall apart in front of Bristol.

"Please don't panic my sweet one, I will now be able to watch over you. If you're somehow free from my physical grasp, I will be able to track you down. Your emotions are my emotions, and vice versa. I didn't think capturing you would be so easy."

The pit of my stomach twisted as he slowly slid a finger across my collar bone and up my neck to my cheek.

"Sweet child, you are not my only concern. I have many other vendettas to be taken care of. I despise the elder race." His finger stopped caressing my face then. Bristol sighed deeply before continuing on. "And he was all I could taste in your blood when I bit your neck. As glad as I am to have you here now my queen, knowing that he is present in your blood disgusts me, and makes me want to rip your throat out. However, to proceed with my plan you are a necessity.

"As the days went on I decided from then that I wanted to right old wrongs, and it just so happened that the elder race was a major wrong. To rid the world of the ridiculous rule or show the humans what a real vampire is.

"And now I have you. If you choose correctly then all will end well, and if you choose incorrectly then death will come to you and those you love. Plus I will tell the humans of us and ruin any peace between the races. You have a very big decision to make."

I will drain her of her blood.

What the hell? I had heard Bristol's thoughts. I forgot that if he could hear my thoughts, then that means I can hear his. Panic rose in me, and I was trying so hard to hide it from him. He had said he would keep me alive if I chose his side.

"Your full intention is just to kill me. Isn't it?"

"Where did you hear that in the lovely speech I gave? I will save you if you choose to be by my side."

"No. That's not what you're thinking."

"Oh dear. You caught me. Your blood, all of it, will bring back my sanity. Also with your precious life's source, I would gain unimaginable powers. Far greater than any other vampire out there. So yes, my plan is to drain you completely dry." Laughter burst from Bristol's mouth.

I sat bound and tied to this chair unable to move or get away. I attempted to push down the bubble of fear that filled me but all in all I was terrified.

* * * * * * * * * *

I could sense the sun coming up outside. My body felt very heavy with exhaustion. I didn't want to sleep but I knew my strength was waning as well. Bristol had left some time ago. The only way I could move anything so far is by seeing it, and obviously my vision was obstructed by the ridiculously large blindfold wrapped around my head covering my eyes. So not even my telekinesis would work right now.

My head drooped and within what felt like seconds I passed out. I immediately fell into a dream. Instead of being in the middle of the woods near a scary dilapidated cabin, I was dropped onto the couch in the mansion. The same comforting leather couch I had many times lounged in.

"You are alive!" My head shot up as I saw Cryder standing in the archway between the foyer and the living room of the house? He came running to me and held me in his arms. I felt tears dripping down my chin, and his body jerked with sobs. "Oh Rena, I have been torturing myself wondering if you were dead or alive still. Where are you? How are you? What is going on? Does Bristol have you? Can you get away?" He bombarded me with a million questions and gave no time in between to answer them.

I wrapped my fingers around his lips to keep him from asking anymore questions, and let him take a deep breath. "I'm...fine. As fine as I can be right now. Yes it's Bristol who has me, and I'm tied up right now to a chair. He has been talking about a plan he's been waiting to use for the last who knows how many years to face up against the elder race. I am being used as his secret weapon. He wants to let humans know we're real. I heard his thoughts and he wants to drain me dry for my powers so he can control the world. Doesn't that sound so cartoonish?"

Cryder's eyes went as wide as a full moon. He listened to everything I told him, and then a growl escaped from his throat. He started shaking his head. "No there is no way you will be involved with any of this. Do you know where you are?"

It was my turn now to shake my head. "I have no clue. I smelled pine trees on the way to wherever he took me, but other than that I am blindfolded."

Cryder continued to hold me close, and I was completely fine with that. I would have been fine if we were stuck like that for the rest of eternity. His warm taut body along with the scent that overpowered all of my senses, which me feel like I had died and gone to heaven.

He stared into my eyes searching my soul, then he grabbed my hands in his and pressed them to his heart. "I want to tell you this, and never have you question my intentions. Everything I have done comes from the heart. Whether to fight for you or take care of you or only be there by your side, it is all from my heart. I love you Rena. Truly love you."

I couldn't tell if it was his heart that was racing or mine, or if they were pounding at the same pace. I had waited so long to hear those words. "You what?"

"I love you. Not only that but I am in love with you. There is no one that is more perfect for me than you are. You helped me find my humanity. You make me laugh, which I have not done in forever. You make me want to live. You are not only my bond-mate, you are my soul mate."

My heart threatened to beat through my chest as I said the words I had felt for him since the first time I saw him. "Cryder it is only you and me, it will always be only you and me. I couldn't imagine feeling more complete around anyone else but you. I love you too." I didn't realize I was crying until I felt the warm wetness sliding down my cheeks.

He then wrapped his arms around my waist and brought me closer to him. He had a smile on his face, and I realized I had wrapped my own arms around his neck. Our faces were inches away from each other. His sweet hot breath caressed my face, and I had to keep reminding myself to breath.

"I love you my guardian, my bond and soul mate, and my king," I whispered into his lips, and then kissed him again.

He pulled away from the kiss. "I will find you my love. I will not let you stay with him much longer, and you will not be any part of his disturbing plan. He will pay for kidnapping you and for every other awful thing he has done."

As much as I loved having him there to protect me and be my knight in shining armor, I knew I had to keep him away from Bristol. "Cryder you can't. You can't come for me. I'll find my way to you. But I couldn't stand to know that you were in danger. He said he would kill you all if I went against him,and I couldn't deal if I was the one that caused you all to be in danger. Please listen to me." He opened his mouth to argue against all of my comments, I was sure of that, but I sped on with my words and kept pleading my case. "I will come up with something. This is my fight, he is my battle. Remember I love you, and I will see you when this is all over." With tears in my eyes threatening to burst through like a dam about to break, I pulled back from his arms and pinched myself to wake up.

I woke with a start in the same rotted place, and still tied up and blindfolded. I could feel myself trembling from the dream I had with Cryder, and knew I needed to get a hold of myself. A plan had to be created.

The slimy slithering voice that came out of nowhere made me jump. "Are you feeling hungry yet dear one? I would not mind feeding you personally. Straight from the vein is always much tastier. But I guess you already know that." He said this as he slowly rubbed the now almost perfectly healed puncture wounds in my neck.

My heart ached for Cryder all over again, but I straightened up making sure I was blocking all thoughts.

"Well I guess no response is a no. You will have to suffer then."

The thought of tasting blood again made my mouth water, but I let that thought and those urges slide out as quickly as possible. I had to fight past this part of my change, I couldn't let it control me. "I'm fine." I said through gritted teeth.

"We will see how fine you are within a few days of not feeding. I know your body requires large quantities of blood right now. You will be begging me for a drop soon enough." His footsteps came closer, and my body stiffened. His hand clasped my chin, hard. He tilted my face up and before I knew it his lips crushed mine with such ferocity.

I pulled away quickly, wanting to spit, or puke sounded better.

He chuckled, and I wished my hands were free so I could have socked him square in the jaw. "It may seem unpleasant now, but that too will change soon. Your feelings for me will be different soon, very very soon." A chair scooted across wooden floors, and he now sat to my right. "I believe it's my turn to taste you. It's been so long since the last time, and my hunger is returning with a strong force." His hand slithered to my shoulder down my arm to untie the ropes that bounded my hands behind my back.

I struggled against his pull on the ropes, not wanting to feel his fangs on any part of my body.

"Do not fight me. You won't win, and this is your part in the fight against the elder race. You will be my blood source."

My mouth went instantly dry, and my body froze. "What?" My lips felt numb then, and that one word barely oozed out.

"Your blood already carried the pure-blood gene before you met Cryder, but now that your blood has infused with his, it is powerful. Any who drink from you will gain great strengths. I think I may keep you around a little longer and draw it all out slowly. No need to rush. I will become like a god and you will be my consort. It will be a beautiful relationship." There was a far away sound to his voice, he was daydreaming of this ridiculous plan. He really thought his bullshit of a plan would work.

I wouldn't let it. "I would rather die than spend another moment with you, you monster," I screamed as loud as I could. I heard a popping noise, and a yelp from Bristol.

"Oh are you angry my dear?" Bristol shuffled his feet. "It looks like we will be sitting in the dark thanks to your anger issues. I am shocked to know that you have power like this, and yet you've sat there silently this whole time without trying to come at me. I guess my blood in you is working faster that I had anticipated."

Vomiting, that's what I felt like doing right then. I wasn't going to tell him the only reason I've been sitting here is because I can't control my power. I was willing to let him think anything he wanted by that point. I could hear different noises around me. Bristol cleaned up whatever mess I created. The noises slowly drifted away, and I hoped he had left to go sleep or do whatever evil-vampires-who-want-to-take-over-the-world do in their spare time.

That hope was short lived as I felt a hand come down against my cheek. "And you will never call me a monster again. Those words are hurtful dear."

My cheek burned from his slap. I had never been hit before and holy shit did it hurt like hell. Bristol then moved his hand down to my arms and started to untie my knots again. I was too shocked to fight against him this time, my cheek still felt like it was being held over an open flame, and the pain from him moving my arms after being behind my back this whole time was agonizing. I wanted to scream out, but I didn't want to give him the pleasure of hearing me in pain. I sat there as he finally untied all of the ropes and released my arms.

I felt a warm rush of relief, concern, and vengeance. One thing I didn't want, something that I tried so hard to prevent from happening was happening now. I wanted to deny the feelings my body was washed with. Maybe they were my own, they weren't being sent to me. I distinctly remember telling him that this was my fight. I didn't want anyone trying to find me, or put themselves in harm's way.

I was being enveloped in strong emotions of love, and some calming vibes. By the strength of each ounce of emotion being sent to me, I knew with the fullest sense of fear that Cryder was near. He was headed straight for the cabin, straight for me, and plummeting into the arms of danger.

I sat up stiffly in the chair. I wanted to get out of the cabin before he made his way, and came face to face with Bristol again. I should've known he wasn't going to listen to me when I told him to stay away, but I'd hoped it would take him a long time to find me. Something sharp being sliced through my skin brought me out of my wandering thoughts.

Bristol squeezed the skin together that he'd cut through. My blood dribbled out of the wound. I had to blink a million times before I could really take in what was going on. He had lowered his head toward my arm, and as I sat there I felt his tongue snake across my bleeding flesh. Everything moved in slow motion like the pause button had been pushed.

"Yesssss." A hiss of a word escaped from his lips as he lapped up every last drop that drained from the shallow wound he had created in my forearm. "I needed it. I can't wait any longer. Power is surging through me. I can feel it crackle through my bones. Her blood is important. I need the power. Don't make me wait any longer. A little taste can not hurt, much." He wasn't talking to me.

I sat there for a few moments putting together a plan while he drank my blood. I felt another scratch along my upper arm this time, and sucked in a breath so that I wouldn't scream. His hand wrapped near the freshest wound, and he sucked in a slight intake of breath and knew he was about to go for my blood again.

This was it, the break I had waited for. I needed to get out of here and now was my moment. I had to get away before Cryder made his way here, before I was drained completely of blood, and out of hope for survival.

Chapter 15

Bristol's rotted breath warmed the crook of my neck. I had no other chance but this. I forced my left hand into a tight ball, letting my training kick in. I braced myself and pulled my arm back then forced it forward in one swift vampire motion. I thought that I had missed and hit air until I felt bones crack under my knuckles.

A loud ear piercing scream came from Bristol. A crash as he fell, and then a few popping and cracking noises as he put his face back together.

I pulled the blindfold off and squinted against the overhead light. Searching the room to find Bristol, I came across a bloodied heap slouched against a wall across the room from me. Bristol had blood dripping from his nose, which was broken, and his skin hung loosely from his face. Vampire strength came in handy, especially when you needed to fight off a vile-piece-of- shit trying to drink your blood to gain crazy powers.

He glanced up at me from his spot on the ground, and a hiss escaped his lips. I glanced around the building and realized that he had taken me to in my dreams.

"Why would you show me the place you were planning on bringing me to?"

"This is my home," he rasped out.

"Well now you won't be able to hide you idiot." I sent images to Cryder.

"You bitch, do you really think one punch would stop me?" He stood then.

"No I didn't. I may have moments of being completely stupid but...I got this. Trust me." I turned toward him. Ripping the arm of the old rocking chair off, I sprinted at full speed and buried the stick into his chest.

"That isn't going to...kill...me" He choked out.

"No, but if I have learned something it's that you are feeling very sleepy right about now." I smiled at him as he collapsed to the ground. "I want this to be the face you remember as you lay here and rot you bastard." I wouldn't be the helpless girl any more, I wouldn't. I will be the vampire queen.

The blood that flows through my veins would be freed. I didn't stop for one stupid second after that. I ran.

Darkness filled the sky, I couldn't see stars or the moon, it was just dark. My vampire vision allowed me to see every tree, bush, and preying animal in my path. Everything around was a blur, and yet I could distinguish through it all. I wanted to stop to see if I could find my way out of this maze of a forest, but my legs continued to push me straight ahead like they knew where to go.

Within minutes of sending the images, I felt knocked down by a strong sense of relief and love given by Cryder. To know that I would soon be in his arms made me run faster. He would find me, and we could go home. The crisp air clung to my face. Out of nowhere a bright blinding light covered my vision. I had to stop.

My eyes adjusted themselves and found a human figure shimmering out of thin air standing in front of me. It went from a mist into a solid shape. A woman bathed in light stood before me now. She was the most beautiful lady I had ever seen. Having her in front of me, I felt a need to run to her. I wanted to hug her, have her proud of me. But I couldn't move.

Her long raven hair spiraled down to her ankles. It twirled back and forth with the wind tossing and flipping it. Her eyes glowed brighter than anything I had seen before, they were gold. Her lips were pursed together forming a heart the color red. She stood there in a long all white flowing gown, arms hanging loosely at her sides, and her eyes casually watched me as I took her appearance in.

The instant I noticed her looking at me I gulped loudly. A smile formed on her beautiful face. With that warm smile, my heart beat faster and her beauty went from amazing to radiant. There was nothingness around us, only the bright light she had appeared to me in. As we stood a moment longer, she stretched out her arm and beckoned me to come closer. I did, without any hesitation.

I stood before her, she again gestured but this time for me to take a seat on the ground. I did. She sat down in front of me and held that extravagant smile in place. The smile made me feel loved and protected. A question started to form on my lips but I paused, too nervous to speak.

Finally after a few more seconds of silence, she spoke, "Hello Rena." Her voice was lower than I expected, but filled with full power and femininity.

The sound alone sent a shiver through me, and I again felt protected and washed from head to toe with love. Hearing those two words had me closing my eyes and accepting the adoration and the warmth of her tone.

"H-how could this be?" Tears fell from my eyes. She smiled an even more glorious smile.

"Hi my sweet child. I have missed you so much."

"How could you be here right now?"

"You needed me. I came. I have been watching over you, and wished that there had been more time before to explain everything to you. Right now my focus is on making sure you follow the path with which you are meant to follow."

"Path? I have a path?"

"You are a destined queen Rena. Your powers are greater than most, and will only grow when you take your seat at the throne. When you accept your place you will complete the ritual and take your rightful spot in life. That is what you are meant for and that is I, along with the family you surround yourself with will be fighting for."

I sniffled. "But it's you. You're here."

She nodded. "I know it's a lot to take in, but I'm here to guide you. Bristol's plan against the elder race and against vampires isn't finished. You still have more to face with him and a bond to be severed."

"There's more to fight? What if I'm not strong enough? Bristol showed me my future, two possibilities. Both looked grim."

An angelic laugh flowed from her mouth. "Do not fret the images of the futures that were played before you. They were merely a ploy for you to choose sides with Bristol. He had hoped you would choose to survive over love and death. However you went against him instead. He is weak compared to what you will face in the future."

"He's weak? It's going to get worse?"

"Yes, but don't fear. For now, you must worry about finding the real you inside, the woman that has been trying to break free. The one I started and now it is up to you to finish. I love you my sweet child, Rena. I'm always watching over you, always have been. Seek me for help when you feel you have failed and unable to stand. I will be there. I'm always on your shoulder. I miss you and love you my dear Rena." And with those last words, she lifted her hand to stroke my cheek.

I closed my eyes as she leaned forward and pressed her soft motherly lips to my forehead. When I opened my eyes, she had gone. Tears fell like waterfalls off my cheeks.

"I love you too, mom."

The white bright light vanished as well, and I was back in the dark dreary forest. Seeing her and hearing her powerful words left an impact in my chest. I was to be queen, to rule the elder race, and create a civilization that is filled with love and strength. There were no options to lay down and give up, so I wouldn't. I ran at full speed again.

This time I knew where to go. I could feel it calling me. This place knew I would be coming, it had warned me ahead of time that this would happen, and now I was ready. I broke free through the trees like the sun exploding through a cloudy day.

The forest behind me evaporated as my breath was stolen by the image before me. I ended up exactly where I had intended to go, but forgot how absolutely beautiful this place was. The rainbow of flowers swayed gorgeously with the breeze even with the only light shining on them was from the moon. I could see them dancing back and forth. The same rocks that had been sitting there in the dream, sat in the same spot now.

The large boulder that my butt would be resting on soon enough had its jagged edges on the sides jutting out like a million tiny knives ready to strike. Everything to the exact detail was laid out before me, and I knew that the field from my dream had called out to me because it was time for me to face my fear. Face the evil that followed me. As I stood in the middle of the field now, enjoying the glorious view that it cast out, I sensed Cryder nearby. He stood on the opposite side of where I was. He only stared at me, watching me, a mixture of emotion rippled through his face. I saw love, amazement, relief, fear, and happiness all at once. I felt a rush of joy from him, and I reveled in it. But I didn't want him there. It was my fight, even my mom had said it, he was in more danger for being there.

I stayed still as a statue in the middle of the field and tried to come up with what to say to make this better, or easier for him. But I couldn't. He would have to understand, and that's exactly how I approached it.

"Cryder," I shouted. "Don't move. Don't come out here. I need to learn to be queen. Let me try, please?"

Cryder's blue eyes glowed as bright as the full moon that was shining down on us. In that second I could see every ounce of emotion he felt. His respect for me and understanding my decision glistened around him.

He nodded ever so slightly. "As you wish my love." He turned and headed back into the forest.

Even though I had told him to go, my stomach knotted to see him walk away, but I knew it was for the best. To continue the balance between vampires and humans, I couldn't die or the equality that had taken many years to accomplish would end.

Twigs cracking behind me killed the silence. The ache in my stomach ended my short-lived moment of peace sensing Bristol behind me. Our blood bond extended its long fingers and connected us as we found each other again in the clearing.

"Well, we know that stakes don't hold for long on you." I shrugged and whipped around, feeling the power surge through every cell of my being.

I was ready to face my fate.

Staring into the eyes of evil, I knew this fight needed to be fought for a civilization that would fall apart without the king and queen. I wouldn't be the strong queen without facing something that weakened me. Cryder and I needed to bring back life to the elder race. I couldn't let them down.

"You can give in you know? We don't need to take it this far." Bristol's words slithered slowly to my ears.

"Are you saying you will walk away from all of this? You'll vanish off the face of the earth and never come back?"

"I wouldn't ever agree to that." His laughter exploded through the silence of the field. "What I would agree to is if you gave up now, and let me use your blood to actually do something great with it."

I shook my head. My lips curled in a sneer.

"Let me tell you this," I took a deep breath. "This," I gestured at both of us, "is between you and me. I will not run from you or run with you. Your plans are just plain dumb. I do know that I'll put it all on the line to keep you from leaving this clearing conscious."

My heart was thudding loudly in my ears. My breath came out in fast puffs.

Fear came and went on Bristol's face. As quickly as it was there it was gone.

He stood for a few more seconds then he took one step closer toward me. "Humans are mere animals, and the weak vampires that stand back and do nothing for this earth are no better. None of them deserve to live, but I will let them all live. I will teach the vampires how to survive as they are meant to, and to show them how to rise up against all. And I'll keep the humans alive as our herd, our pets, to feed on. It will be beautiful. It'll go back to the way this world was originally meant to be."

"Ugh. Blah...blah...blah. I'm tired of hearing this story over and over. I get it, okay? Find someone that cares, because you're boring me."

"Oh you little whore. How dare you speak to me that way."

I shrugged, a very exaggerated shrug, and made my way over to the big boulder that had been waiting for me to take a seat on it. My movements were graceful, and everything was falling into place.

"I will drink your blood, drain you of your power, and end the balance you're wholeheartedly trying to keep. It will all end today," Bristol continued.

This time I laughed. I wanted him to see that his threats weren't intimidating. His threats to kill baited me more into fighting him rather than running away. I wanted him to feel like a lesser being.

"I may not be able to kill you but I will be able to over-power you. Trust me."

"I like how you're trying to be brave in front of me sweet one. But you have forgotten that I have tasted your sweet blood, which means I can feel the tension taking over your body even when you speak those hateful words," he said with a wave of dismissal.

I gulped loudly. How was I going to win this? I couldn't control my powers. How did I expect to walk away alive? Truth: I didn't.

So I blinked hard trying to force the fear down and hopped off the boulder to stare Bristol directly in his soulless eyes. "Say what you want. I don't care. You're annoying me. Give it a rest already and let's get this bullshit over with."

A low rumbling growl escaped from his throat, and a snarl formed on his lips like a rabid dog. "Oh you hateful bitch. I am tired of your rude comments. I would rather rid the world of you now than have you near me any longer. I can not wait to sink my fangs into you once again. You will die tonight." His snake like hissing voice transformed into that of a snarling grisly bear.

He was ready to fight, I felt the same. His over grown body trembled with anger, and I didn't have long to wait before he attacked.

Bristol rushed at me with full vampire speed. I was able to follow his movements, and dodge as he leaped with his arms stretched out to capture me. I spun around in time to see him coming at me a second time, except he had a fist out aimed for my face. As he moved closer I whipped my arm back and with as much force as I could put into it, I punched him. He collapsed to the ground and I could smell his blood weaving itself through the air. The strong smell of it made my mind fog up and my mouth water. My fangs slid from my gums and every where that I looked I saw red. My anger over-powered the blood, and I felt nothing but hatred for the vampire that stood before me.

Bristol took his chance to come at me and tackled me to the ground. I fell face first in the grass as his body straddled over me. He pulled my hands behind my back. I screamed out and he pulled harder.

Bristol flipped me over, and his face hung mere inches away from mine. He pushed my arms above my head as his body still straddled my own. Looking straight into his eyes I could only feel dread bottling up inside of me. The end of everything would happen soon. I knew I couldn't last much longer against him. I was no match for him, and knew that I would fail.

I could feel warm wetness dripping down the side of my face as I lay on my back looking into nothingness. He was about to end me and so I turned my head to expose my neck. I shouldn't fight it any longer.

I heard a low guttural laugh coming from Bristol. His hot breath clawed its way to my neck. His dark mess of hair fell forward covering us like a curtain, and his fangs scraped across my skin.

The vein in my neck that he drooled over pulsed erratically making it obviously visible for him. This vein would deceive me soon and give itself over to him. I squirmed under his body trying to break free, but it was no use. So I laid there, shutting my eyes tight in anticipation for the sharp pain that would take over my whole body when his fangs fully pierced through. This was it. My life's source would be drained from me, darkness and death would come next enveloping me in their pain free arms. I wasn't afraid, I didn't resist. In fact I welcomed it.

I laid waiting to be bitten when Bristol's body was tossed from mine. I heard a few snarls and growls before I decided to look. Cryder had attacked him and now they were fighting each other. Cryder paused enough from the fight to turn and look at me. "His...eyes. That's his power."

With those words I snapped out of the trance...trance? Has it happened before?

Those empty black pits for eyes held some power. How could I have not known that?

"Get the hell away from him Bristol." The red fog came back.

"Rena, don't do this. We need to fight together." Cryder said from beside Bristol.

I shook my head. "Not now. I can't now. This has to be finished."

Bristol took a step toward me and Cryder blocked his path. "Fight me." He said to Bristol.

"I want her. She will give me what I need." Bristol kept his gaze on me.

I stared in his eyes, but this time nothing happened. Now that I knew I could control myself. "Leave, Cryder. Please."

"I can't."

"Very well." I twitched my wrist toward the woods, and Cryder followed that exact path as he was tossed from the open field.

I didn't give a second thought to him and turned on my heels. The large comfy boulder called my name, and so I followed.

"Falling to my level are we?"

I stared into his eyes not feeling an ounce of any type of emotion toward him except rage. My body had turned cold, but the blood that flowed in my veins boiled. I could feel that power. The one growing inside of me since day one, and it waited on my command. The crackle of the power in my fingertips felt like hundreds of tiny electric shocks running through my hands. The wind wrapped its caressing tendrils around me in eager anticipation. My hair fluttered around my body. "No one could fall that low Bristol. You belong in hell, and that's where I'm sending you."

It was then that I gave in to my nature. Raising my hands to the beautiful uncontrollable sky above me that belonged to mother nature, I closed my eyes and ears to the world. "Oh true goddess, give me strength." Quietly I whispered, "Mother help me now. Show me who I am. Help me to be in control," I whispered.

A strong sense of love and comfort filled me. When I opened my eyes, my body glowed with a beautiful golden hue and I levitated off the ground. My body continued to glow as I tore my eyes from the beauty and turned them to Bristol. With nothing but hatred I told the stones near him to lift up and attack.

Hitting him in the head, blood immediately gushed from his wound.

This time I demanded bigger rocks to fly and inflict him with as much pain as he caused us. Again they obeyed and rose together to attack Bristol. He ran from them, screaming, as one at a time they slashed into his body. I felt satisfaction with listening to his screams grow louder, and his blood wafted through the air.

Hysterical laughter exploded from me, which surprised me to hear it at all, as I watched Bristol run like a chicken with his head cut off.

"Run, run as far away as you can, because if you stay here with me it will only get worse...for you." My voice chimed in my ears like tinkling bells.

He stopped and turned to face me with a snarl on his lips. "Don't threaten me. You think these cheap parlor tricks will stop me?"

I shrugged.

He took a few steps in my direction, pausing a brief moment and watching me carefully with a mild look of fear careening through his eyes. He forced himself forward with large powerful strides. His chest puffed up like a blow-fish, as if he was about to fight a hundred men instead of me.

His speed began to increase, and when he was only a few inches in front of me I let the full power of my voice command him. "Stop!"

With that one word his body froze.

"You stupid girl. What have you...done to me?"

I laughed. "Can't you just accept that you're defeated? I win you lose. I'm tired of this crap."

"I...will...drain...you."

"*If* you can get free."

He moved slightly making low gurgle noises. This wasn't over.

I backed up into the sharp boulder that sat dead center of the field and ran my hands up the pointy sides. I asked the sword-like stems that jutted out from the big rock to break apart and aim themselves at the monster. I envisioned the sharp daggers flying across the field at Bristol's next move. To cut off the monster coming to attack us, and find his heart.

The glow to my skin came back bright as ever, as I prepared myself for the next step.

Bristol's body tore free from my hold and I asked the rock-edged knives to follow through. They listened. Bristol stopped short of taking his giant leap to me. His hands went to his chest, his eyes as wide as saucers, and his blood quickly stained the front of his shirt. His once white tee was now only red.

Within seconds Bristol's eyes lolled back into his head, as he stumbled backwards to the ground. Blood poured from his mouth and gurgles took over his breathing. I fell to my knees beside him. I had never killed before.

"Re...na," Bristol rasped.

I blinked away tears for the monster that laid before me. "Don't speak Bristol. It will only make it worse. Let the coma take over."

"Re...na," he whispered again. "Clo...ser."

"Sssshhh we're going to take you somewhere that you won't be able to hurt yourself or anyone ever again. Rest."

"...will kill you. I will...kill your friends. I'll be...back."

I saw red. The aroma of his blood was delicious, but it also reminded me that he wanted to kill everyone I loved, and that his hold on me would only get stronger if I didn't end him now. The breeze lifted my hair. I closed my eyes and pictured an invisible hand reaching from my glowing body into Bristol's black soul. Where his heart slowly beat that invisible hand wrapped around it. Held it until it stopped.

I glared into Bristol's black holes. They widened with fear when he felt his heart being forced to stop. "You won't kill anyone ever again, Bristol. I'm done with you," I growled. "You won't come back. You feel that around your heart? That's my power, my rule. I'm queen and I sentence you to death."

The invisible hand didn't let go of the heart, but squeezed tighter until a loud pop came from behind his ribs. Bristol's body convulsed and then soon stopped. Everything stopped for him. His breathing, his moving, and his ability to hurt others.

We'll be safe now, right? I did the right thing. I think.

"Oh my goddess you're alive," Cecile's shouts brought me out of the scary thoughts my mind kept screaming at me. "I've been so worried. Cryder said you were here, in the field still with Bristol, and so we came to find you...Cryder was in the trees, but you were here."

"It...was...my...fight."

She hugged me. "Right. It was...oh holy hell. What happened to..."

"He threatened to kill us. His heart...it..."

"Sssshhh don't worry about it. We'll talk about it later. Let it out, Ren."

Tears soaked my t-shirt and sobs poured from my throat. "Is Cryder...is he mad at me?"

"Mad? Oh no. Girl he is not mad. He said you did what you had to do. Maybe a little too forceful, but you aren't in full control. It's fine. We can all work on it together."

"Is he hurt?"

"He's injured and needs to be fed, but other than that he will be healed quickly." Drake startled me as he walked up behind us. "I'm going to get rid of the asshole."

Cecile led me to where Cryder waited.

"I could never be mad at you. You are a true goddess, a true queen. You fought for the safety of your family. How can I be mad?" The awe in his voice made my stomach sink.

"I sent you away. I really wanted you near me, but you weren't suppose to be there. I...I killed him...with my..." Tears threatened again.

Cryder took my chin in his soft hand and turned my face so that I was looking into his amazing crystal blue eyes. "You did what needed to be done. That's all. You are amazing."

Drake came running to us. "Cryder, he's gone."

"What do you mean?" Cryder asked.

"How can he be gone? Rena killed him," Cecile said.

I gulped.

Drake took us to where Bristol's body had been. "There's a path of where he drug himself away or something got to him. But he's not in the clearing."

Where Bristol's dead body had been there was only a large puddle of blood.

"He couldn't have gotten up by himself...right?" I questioned, feeling my knees going weak.

Cryder shook his head.

"I failed after all."

Cryder pulled me to him, and I laid my head on his chest feeling knots the size of baseballs floating in my stomach. "You weakened him. We'll be able to find him before he finds us."

I didn't want to remind Cryder that Bristol's blood flowed through my veins now. I could track him and he could find me. It was *my* blood he needed to heal now that we were bonded.

I didn't know what it would take to really defeat him. How to stop him from following through with his plan, but I vowed to myself right then that I would learn to hone my powers and be the vampire queen.

My promise to all of them, as well as myself: the next time Bristol and I come face-to-face, he would be begging for death. I had a lot more to live for, to fight for, a vampire race that expected a lot from me. These were my people, my friends and family, that depended on me. If it was a battle Bristol wanted, then a battle Bristol would get. I would be prepared.

Epilogue

*The next night...

Cryder brought me even closer to him, and I felt comfy and safe in his arms. Every breath I took was filled with the wonderful aroma of the wilderness. His woodsy sweet scent reminded me of home. He leaned his face toward me, and then his lips were on mine. Crushed against my mouth with a deep passion that I had never felt before.

With an obvious intense hunger, his kisses were all I could feel or think about. They filled my mind and my body with the most amazing pleasure. I couldn't stop myself from letting little moans escape in between each one.

His hands roamed my body and everywhere he touched he left flames all over my body. Even in places he didn't touch I could feel the heat traveling. I found it hard to breath, but at that moment I didn't care if I ever took a breath again. With him was where I wanted to stay.

I never wanted his kisses to stop. And I never wanted to leave the safe cocoon of his body. I knew if death took me right then, that I would die insanely happy.

I ended up with my back on the bed, and Cryder looked down at me. My fingers traced every defined line of his naked, smooth, chiseled chest. Naked?

I didn't know how that happened but I wasn't complaining. Our kisses become more intense, and his lips were on mine gently prying my mouth open to let his tongue search my mouth. A loud moan escaped from me and led to him wrapping an arm around my back to pull me closer into him. We couldn't get close enough. If our bodies molded in to each other, I still couldn't say that would be close enough.

His tongue slid from my mouth down to my neck, and shivers convulsed through my body. Tingles took over running through my stomach and to the up-until-now-non-existent areas. I wanted him bad. His hands explored up my shirt, and when his hand found my chest, new girly sounds escaped my throat. He massaged my breasts, and I felt like I could explode into a zillion pieces of pure pleasure.

I could tell very easily that Cryder was at the same point as me. He pulled me to him and let his body melt into mine. Our minds and bodies moved together. He penetrated my neck deeply with his sharp fangs, and an animal growl escaped my lips. I couldn't hold back long enough before I sank my fangs into the dark vein on his neck.

And then there were fireworks.

* * * * * * * * *

"How are you feeling now?" I asked, trying to catch my breath. Lying next to me, Cryder held a large smile.

"I feel much better now. Definitely better," he chuckled. "Your blood tastes different though."

I was in the middle of stretching and stopped immediately, worry filled my voice. "Why? What do you mean?"

"I can't tell what it is. There's more power in it, that's why I was able to heal quicker than normal. But there was something extra that didn't taste right."

Was this a test? Had he not heard the conversation Bristol and I had? I didn't want to mess up anything good.

I would tell him later. "Maybe it's that my powers are growing?" He shrugged. Changing topics. "My mom came to me in a vision."

"Oh yeah?"

"Yeah she wanted to warn me of my future. That I would have a big battle to face, and that it was only going to get harder. But she's proud of me at least." I shrugged.

I should be more worried about an impendable doom, but I wasn't.

"Why wouldn't she be? You're extraordinary."

"Whatever."

Cryder planted his lips on mine. "Just trust us."

"Oh so now you're siding with my mom? You've never even met her."

"Well we agree on this," he laughed.

"Glad to know," I giggled.

* * * * * * * * * *

"I'm glad that you two were able to have some alone time, and it's good to see Cryder has his healthy glow again." Cecile grinned over at him, then winked in my direction. "Welcome to the dark side girly."

I rolled my eyes and leaned into Cryder, who sat as close as possible to me on the couch. His woodsy scent floated to my nose, and I inhaled. I never wanted to be without that aroma or his warm body.

Cecile was draped over Drake's lap like an over-sized rag doll, so relaxed, and almost as if she didn't realize that we all almost died yesterday.

If Bristol had been able to get to me. Or if my powers hadn't worked, and if I would have given in completely. He would have bitten me. Then the vampire race would be doomed and basically all put to death.

Drake leaned forward, his brow furrowed in serious concentration as he spoke, "what happens now?"

I glanced up at Cryder, waiting for his response, but his focus was on me searching for an answer. I turned back to Drake to see he was also looking at me.

"Why are you two looking at me?"

"You ended the plan of one of our craziest rogues. I will look to the two of you for my answers, I won't ever doubt you. My king and queen." Drake then bowed his head to us.

I glanced at Cryder as he bowed his head and I did the same.

"Right now, I guess we'll lay low for a few days. Relax, and recuperate. Once we have healed mentally and physically, we'll move on to finding Bristol," I said.

"From the brief description he gave to Rena. His plan is to go after vampires and humans alike, however I think he will try to attack the elder race first. He wants to be above the vampires first, I know this because he wants to feel like he has the most power. Between humans and vampires, we are the strongest." Cryder continued. "I believe he may try to recruit other rogues, like himself, to begin the war between the two races. So we're going to have to find him first before he gains too much strength. We can't have him beating us with numbers."

"Where do you think he will retreat to first?" Drake asked pointedly at Cryder.

"He'll go where the rogues have made themselves a nest. A safe-house, so to speak. The last I heard of their location, they were hiding out in some middle of nowhere country area in Tennessee."

"So that's where we're going I'm guessing?" Cecile asked.

"Looks like it. Road trip here we come," I said holding back as much sarcasm as I could.

There was no excitement in knowing we would be trying to find Bristol. I'd been hoping that I could wait patiently until he came for me again, but I knew Cryder was right. Remembering his words from the cabin, he wouldn't stop until he reached the top.

"Well then let's relax. I seriously have some much needed beauty rest to catch up on. And by looking that three of you, I would say you all could use some too." Cecile laughed, and we all gave her our very own 'go to hell' looks. "Oh calm down and take those looks off your face. Lack of sleep makes you all grumpy. "

Ignoring Cecile, Drake spoke, "Cryder we have to contact the elder race and let them know what's going on. They may be able to send in reinforcements to help us. I'm sure they will have no problem with sharing a few of their expert shooters considering it's to save the whole race."

"Right Drake. We'll sleep, get rested, then make all the phone calls tomorrow. Right now, there are other things I would like to take care of." Cryder stood up then and gestured for me to take his hand. He helped me off the couch and we headed upstairs.

When he and I reached the doorway of his bedroom, Cryder bent down and hoisted me up into his arms. A little girl's squeal escaped my lips as he cradled my body against his.

Cryder's eyes were golden as he stared into mine, and then placed his soft lush lips gently onto mine. "I love you Rena," he said as he pulled away breathless.

I tried to get my heart rate back to normal when I responded, "I love you too Cryder, with all of my heart."

He took a step over the threshold into his bedroom. Still holding me comfortably in his arms, he nuzzled his nose into my ear and then kissed my earlobe. The feel of his lips on my ear made a shiver flow through my body.

"Do you trust me?" He whispered and his breath tickled my ear.

Goosebumps rose all over my body and the hair on my neck stood up. His lips traced down my ear to my neck and back up. My body felt like jello.

"What do you mean?" I asked breathless.

"Do you trust me yes or no?" This time his tongue glided over the same areas his lips had just touched.

I couldn't breath or even think, all I could manage was a slow half-hearted nod.

This time when he spoke, his voice came out in a deep raspy sound. "Then let me see if I can make you forget your worries."

At that I couldn't think, couldn't concentrate, and for damn sure couldn't speak. He took me further into the bedroom, shutting the door behind him, and lowering me to the bed. As I laid there watching him move around the room lighting candles, I tried to catch my breath.

"You are my life Cryder, I want you to know that. You are my everything. You have to be with me always."

He stopped what he was doing, with a serious look on his face, he made his way toward the bed.

"You are my life too." A smile played on his lips as he leaned over to kiss me again. "You don't know how long I've waited to hear those words come from your mouth my love, my queen."

Book 2:

Struggle With Love

Coming out in late 2012

Will Rena and her friends be able to get rid of Bristol once and for all?

Can Rena fight against the hold Bristol has on her? Will Cryder be able to accept that Rena now has his and Bristol's blood running through her veins?

With Love Series

is on Facebook

ABOUT THE AUTHOR

Tiffany Heiser

is a writer living in Fort Worth, Tx- with her Husband and two crazy dogs. She has been writing most of her life-short stories, and poetry. But she has always enjoyed reading young adult fiction and the amazing places it can take you. It has been her dream to one day be published. Her dream was accomplished with **Bonded With Love** as her debut novel.

You can visit Tiffany online: ***www.tiffanyheiser.com***
Twitter: ***tiffany_heiser***
Visit her blog: ***www.tiffanyheiser.blogspot.com***

Made in the USA
Lexington, KY
30 November 2011